Tower of Babel

Written by: Manuel Delgadillo
Edited by: Kassandra Limon

Contents

Chapter 1

I watched the sunrise outside my window; today's anticipation had kept me awake all night. The fading stars slowed my racing mind for a moment as I saw them dim then disappear. What path would be chosen for me today? What were my next classes? What would I do in this lifetime?

A sense of envy came over me as I looked over at my sleeping classmates. Their path is clear. Even though it hasn't been shown to them, our tests and classes have clearly surfaced their orientated talents. I paused for a moment and looked back at the skyline... "Arrogance." I whispered.

Though I remain a blank slate to myself I'm sure my path is clear to our Levite. This is why the tests were made. This is why I was put through these classes. I'm sure once my path is revealed, the reasons why will be clear to me as well.

The morning bell broke my focus. My questions will be answered soon enough.

Miss. Ivanhiemer was in her usual spot. Our desks and materials were also in their usual location; the only difference was a large stack of packets, which took up most of our teachers' desk. I walked in and took my seat and watched Miss. Ivanhiemer begin passing out the packets.

She began on the end furthest from me. As I watched her, I began to grow anxious; these papers would tell me what I would do for the rest of my life. It will show me who I was in past incarnations and I would hear from myself, first hand, what I have struggled with and the obstacles I have triumphed over.

It was my turn now, but instead of giving me my packet she simply exchanged a glance and continued to the student behind me.

I remained frozen; is this a mistake? Had He not known what to do with me? Is there something wrong with me? Or maybe I was someone with the mark of Cane who had slipped through the cracks. My mind began to race again, when my eyes caught the figure of our director in our class entrance.

Why would the director of this whole floor be here? I thought. In the two years I had spent here I had only seen him once. It was in the group assembly that was held to first acquaint us to the itinerary and rules of this floor.

I didn't notice, but he was looking at me as well. Though his gaze seemed, at the same time, beyond me. My notice seemed to focus his sight. The director stood more firmly and made a gesture with his hand for me to follow him.

Miss. Ivanhiemer was still passing out papers when I stood up from my seat. At that moment everyone's eyes were on me. Everyone's except

Miss. Ivanhiemer; whose attention only darted over to me after each time she placed a packet down.

I walked up to the director and after another broad look in my direction he simply stated, "The Levite wishes to see you." He then began walking.

I was guided down a corridor to a separate building. I had not been in it before but its presence and decorum were similar. As I followed, I watched the line of tile on the wall shift up and down like a snake as we passed by. I had to keep a brisk pace to keep up, which almost caused me to collide with my guide when he finally came to a stop.

My eyes took a moment to adjust when I saw our destination. It was a large red wooden door with unfamiliar carvings and twelve stones embedded in it. It was a sharp contrast to the sterile white and grays I had grown up in. The door seemed ancient. The wood had begun to naturally crack in small areas, which did not mar its appearance but instead gave credit to its age. It seemed almost as if the building was built around it.

My guide, the director, had taken his leave and was making a turn out of sight down the corridor. I stood there for another moment, took a deep breath, and pushed on the door.

Inside were piles upon piles of papers and books. In the center was a thin ancient man scribbling away, adding to the mass of literature, which seemed to hold up the walls themselves.

"Pardon," I said, to make my presence known, but was countered with an upheld skeleton like finger.

So I stood there, waited, and watched the Levite continue his work. I thought, "This is the Levite, our shepherd." Watching him I began to think of the red door as an excellent herald for this man. Out of place and alien, yet their obvious age seemed to predate this building.

He finally stopped, put down his pen, leaned forward and looked me in the eyes.

I hadn't seen his face until this moment and his sudden gaze had startled me. His face was covered with wrinkles and lines, and his skin was a light brown which gave a great contrast to his eyes.

Their color was yellow and his look was matt, unreadable, they expressed nothing. They seemed dead.

He squinted slightly then sat back down. He picked up his pen and watched it as he jumbled it through his fingers.

"Have you read the Bible?" His voice was tactful.

"Yes sir, but it hasn't been translated to me." I tried using my clearest voice.

"What separates mankind from the beasts of this world and the angels of heaven?" He continued watching his pen, as he seemed to practice.

I felt confident with this question. "God gave us dominion over the beasts of this land and has placed us above his angels, so I believe the difference is that we have God's favor."

A small smile cracked across his face. "The difference is choice. An animal can only be an animal. He is driven by basic instinct and self-gratification; he lives dies and has no legacy." He continued with his pen. "An angel can only be an angel they are perfect beings and as such can only be perfect, they live only to serve God; their life is eternal. Mankind is different. They can either be temporal or transcendental..." He smiled once again as he paused. "Through choice."

At that moment a stocky man appeared at the door and the Levite resumed his writing. The man gestured for me to follow him, when I heard the Levite, in an almost satirical tone.

"Your off to learn of mankind's claim to eternity and of God's presence on this earth."

I looked back confused but found him still writing, without a visible expression.

Chapter 2

"Hello Sir." The stocky man's voice fit his form well. His round face was beaming with an unexplainable joy.

"Hello to you, Sir," I replied. It appeared that my confusion was noticeable since the stocky man quickly changed his expression and pulled on his coat, smoothing it a bit and then extended his hand.

"I am Page, Sir. Your retainer." Seeing that my expression still hadn't changed he continued. "I'm here to facilitate and organize your day to day schedule from here on."

His original expression returned and after a moment he muttered to himself, "You don't quite look the same." He paused still staring and whispered. "Maybe." Once again his air of professionalism returned and with a quick: "Follow me please Sir." He began hustling down the hall.

After a good distance from the Levites room we came to a maze of corridors and doors. Page without hesitating continued from one corridor to another, making his necessity perfectly clear. After much traversing we arrived at a very blasé door. Door 528.

"Here we are Sir," said Mr. Page gesturing to me to open the door. After I entered he simply smiled and closed the door behind me.

The room's interior was familiar; it was a duplicate of every other room I had been in, except that of the Levites. There waiting for me was a lanky woman, well in her thirties, but with a beautiful air of poise.

She greeted me with a smile, "I am Debora, your history teacher Sir. You will be skipping a lot of steps you have taken in the past but I am glad I have once again a chance to teach you, Sir."

"You have taught me before Miss.?" It seemed everyone knew more about me than I did.

"Yes, Page, I and everyone in this building has taught and helped you for thousands of years Sir. Some more than others." She pushed her hair off her shoulders with her slender fingers. "You always like to keep yourself in the dark. I never understood why, but I guess it's some kind of inside joke."

She paused and made a small smacking noise with her mouth and continued. "Well, we should get started. This will be a brief condensation of what you would usually have been taught. However the Levite specifically asked for it." With perfect form she pointed at a seat with an open palm.

Puzzled I sat down.

"You do know of the Nuclear War?" Her question was obviously rhetorical.

"Yes, Miss." I still felt compelled to answer.

"Well, what you don't know is what followed afterwards," she paused with a grimace and waved one of her hands in the air. "Yes, I know you were taught about the restructuring of civilization and about the tribes, towns, cities, and infrastructures that arose afterwards. What I mean is you don't know or rather you weren't taught the history of Michael."

It was true. I had heard of Michael, but only as a constant presence. It was part of a brief lesson that involved the mark of Cane and the Elect. We were told that we would later on learn more about their connection with each other, but only after we had received our jobs.

She continued. "Michael was started after the conception of New Jerusalem. You see our predecessors had a new and different problem that hadn't been seen before. Thanks to the Nuclear War, they still had an abundance of technology, but the area they wished to rule was vast and the space between its occupants was large. With limited human resources, their creation for law and structure had to be efficient. That's when Michael's first iteration was widely implemented.

Alpha 1 A1.

It was preexisting technology that was implanted under the skin. It simply told a person's location and served as an accountant and bank for the individual's monetary gains, loses, and purchases. This information was then uploaded to servers.

It wasn't until the ability to monitor a persons vitals was added that Michael really began to form into the tool we know it as today.

With this new form, crime was squashed in a matter of years." At these words she formed a fist. "It was realized that with constant monitoring and with thousands of terabytes uploaded and saved in servers that a chosen few, in a criminal investigation, could simply bring up the information of every individual involved. With Michael they knew everyone's location and vitals during the crime."

Her cheeks started to take on a crimson color. "If someone stole or murdered, Michael's records would be brought up. In the case of a murder, the instant the victim's vitals changed could be pinpointed and paired with the information of everyone who was near by. For theft, a time approximation would be considered along with the items location and the location of those around the area in the suspected time."

Her passion subsided a bit as she slowed down her movements. "In the prevention of crime, the choices for success have been clear since the beginning. Either have consequences so horrendous that though the chances of someone being caught isn't a hundred percent, for most, the image and general brutality of the consequences would remain in people's minds a hundred percent of the time. This would create monsters of those enforcing the law.

"The second choice is the one we have adopted," she held her hands behind her back and slowed her pace. "This choice would be, to have more lenient consequences, but catch those that break the law every time. This second one, as much as societies before us have attempted to accomplish, has not been possible up until these past few thousand years; largely in part to the Levites efforts.

Thanks to sociopaths, conspiracies and more social orientated crimes Michael's form in that time was not capable of catching perpetrators a hundred percent of the time. It could not create the state of learned helplessness we wished for those who sought to challenge the law." She paused and released a deep breath, almost as if letting go of some stirring feeling. "Michael's next evolution could not be done with technology alone, but needed some discoveries in the field of human biology, specifically the brain, pioneered by Dulant.

Michael was lacking more data for such situations in which 'he said she said' was at the center of the problem or when simply hard data was not sufficient to clearly draw a line." She paused again a bit flustered. "Mr. Dulant's research, which he will go over himself, made it possible for Michael to constantly record a persons sense of sight and hearing along with its original capabilities. As a result, Michael's location was moved to the brain." At this almost in melancholy, she took her index finger and touched her forehead.

She turned around and walked closer to me. "We all have Michael in us, except you, but there is another form of Michael that is just as endemic. A result of Dulant's and Page's work. You will learn about that tomorrow."

The mere mention of Mr. Dulant working on Michael seemed to bring her pain, which made me curious. "Excuse me miss but did you invent Michael?"

Her rosy tone returned to her face. "Yes, I was the mother of its conception, or should I say father at that time. I must admit because of my field of work, my contributions to its maturity have been minimal in comparison to others. I was the one to further engineer Michael so that their findings could be implemented, however I could no longer take complete credit." She gave out a small laugh, which lingered as a smile.

"I talk about maturity but the discovery of the human soul evolved Michael into something none of its contributors ever expected... that sums up the short version. You'll understand it more once you talk to Page, Dulant and of course the Levite."

The lesson had gone by a lot quicker than I had expected and it had brought up more questions than it had answers. But, rather than be impatient I simply watched Miss. Debora walk over to the classroom door and open it revealing Mr. Page who signaled me to follow him.

I stood up and began to walk out. "Thank you Miss. Debora." To which she simply smiled as I left.

Mr. Page began to once again navigate through the maze. "I know you have a lot of questions, but you have to see Mr. Dulant tomorrow first before I can speak to you. None of this will make too much sense to you until you speak to the Levite, but he will be the last of us. You will have the treat of seeing Michael tomorrow though."

"Michael? The chip?" This was the only explanation I could think of.

"No, but you will see him tomorrow. Here we are." We had arrived at another door without any special qualities, except that it wasn't numbered. "This is your new room," said Mr. Page as he stopped near the door.

I walked inside. Mr. Page gave me another critical look and closed the door.

I looked around and without much surprise, found the room to be only a smaller version of the room I shared with my classmates; only this one was furnished to accommodate only one.

Stainless steel bed frame, gray walls with white tile floor, cupboard with three shelves and a clock. My window was facing east, just like my previous room. I took a deep breath and exhaled as I walked towards it. Same skyline. Though I could probably see the building where my previous room was from this point, they were all gray duplicates of each other. I quit scanning for distinguishing features and began thinking what was to come. See Michael? The human soul? I was supposed to have gotten answers today not more questions. I began feeling a sense of frustration come over me; they already know what I need to know, why don't they just tell me? I exhaled again. All they have to do is just show me or tell me once.

I shook my head. There has to be a reason they want to do it this way. I looked out the window once again. "Ten trees, I was able to see twelve before. I looked at where my room used to be and laid down on my bed."

I awoke to a tapping at my door. "Time to get ready Sir," it was Page. The lack of sleep from my previous day had affected me. I would have already been up at this hour.

I stood up, rubbed my eyes, and grabbed my fresh clothes from the drawers and walked out. Page pointed at a door across mine. I walked into a smaller redolent shower room and laid out my things as I was taught and began. When I was ready I walked back to my room and placed my previous clothes in the bottom drawer and joined Page who was waiting for me in the hall.

"Where will we be going Sir?" There was much to expect from today.

"To see Michael, then you'll have your explanation from Mr. Dulant and I afterwards." Page began walking at his usual quick pace and I followed him outside.

We went up to one of the vehicles in the rail system that connected our whole city and got on. I had only been on these vehicles a few times before and I was glad to once again have the opportunity to ride on one.

The vehicle began to move and after a few minutes I began seeing a side of the city I hadn't before. Instead of going to a location within its walls we began to take a course that went clearly beyond its limits. This was even better than I could have imagined; a new area away from the gray and whites, away from what had become the mundane and repetitive.

After passing a few walls and checkpoints from above, we began to pass through several trees. Pinus Pinaceae. "What a beautiful smell," I thought. As I looked at our view I saw Mr. Page, stiff and upright simply staring ahead of us at the rails.

"Why is Michael so far from our facility?" It was a legitimate question, but it was more to break the awkward silence.

"Seeing Michael is a privilege. Not anyone can simply see him. Its location was also chosen for the purpose of discretion and so that those affected by him, are not tempted to try something irrational." With that, he pointed to an opening out in the distance.

I couldn't make out much, but I could see a large building with what seemed like an obelisk beside it. As we got closer I began to see that it wasn't an obelisk, but a large statue at the building's entrance.

As soon as I could distinguish its characteristics, I found it to be a beautiful depiction of an angel with a large iron sword in front of him. Its robes had been carved in a way as if they were being blown by a strong wind, with its source being the sword itself. The angel's hair was curled and affected the same way as his robes by the sword. His face had no expression; it simply faced the sword with an indifferent stare. As we got closer I could see that the sword wasn't being held in the angel's outstretched hand, but rather floated near it completely in mid air. The sword was pointing downward and had been heavily corroded by the elements. Its jagged edges seemed to have been sharpened by nature and the pile of oxidized debris on the ground beneath made it look as if the sword had sprang out of the earth and was being presented to the angel.

Another thought came to mind; it also looked as if the angel was releasing his sword into the world by letting corrosion absorb it into the earth.

I looked over and Page's joyful expression reminded me of when I first met him, "Magnificent isn't it? One of your creations." He pulled on his coat once again for a complete reenactment.

Chapter 3

As we pulled up to the buildings entrance an older gentleman began heading in our direction to greet us. He was of medium build with completely white hair; he seemed to be in his mid fifties. As he walked in our direction, I found that his eyes looked as if they were completely closed.

He came up to me first. "I'm Dulant, Sir. It's a pleasure to meet you again. You'll get a tour of Michael, but first we'll use one of its' rooms to go over both Page's and my work." I nodded my head in agreement concentrating mostly on his eyes, which seemed to close even tighter as he smiled.

He then reached over and shook Page's hand. "Mr. Page." His voice was the quintessential tone of professionalism, but a half smile stretched across his face as he said it, giving the gesture a playful contradiction.

Mr. Page stiffened his posture as he received Mr. Dulant's greeting and with an uplifted brow returned, "Mr. Dulant."

Mr. Dulant gave a brief chuckle and began walking past the sentry and towards the building. Mr. Page and I followed.

Midway towards the entrance, Mr. Dulant turned around and began walking backwards. "This is a real treat for us Sir. Mr. Page and I have only seen Michael a few times and without the consent of the Levite." At this he turned back around and outstretched his hands towards the sky. "We would be wiped from existence before we even reached this point." As he finished he grasped the entrances door. He chuckled once again to the clear annoyance of Mr. Page and opened it.

Inside was a confusion of wires, pipes, vents, and noise. Mr. Dulant took a left turn and entered a room with three seats. The walls isolated us from the chaos as the door closed behind us. Both Mr. Dulant and Mr. Page waited for me to take a seat, and then sat down themselves.

"I believe you have the start," said Mr. Dulant facing Mr. Page as he adjusted himself in his seat.

"Yes," said Mr. Page. "My work was in genetics specifically the deciphering of human DNA. It was my curiosity that led to the discovery of the human soul that then prompted the necessity to change Michael to this." He showed no expression and his mannerisms were almost mechanical. "It was my interactions with humans that first set me on my course to finding the human soul. I found that those whom I met and interacted with were sometimes fundamentally the same as others I had met before during my life. At first I assumed that because all humans had the same necessities and because of similar experiences, that it was logical for major flaws and strengths to be shared by others. But I continued finding the same people again and again, so I decided to look into the matter in my spare time from a genetic stand point."

His face looked withdrawn, as if picturing the next steps he took. "We all come from the same pool of codons so it wasn't an irrational thought that genetically there could be another perfect match for someone in the world. Mathematically, the chances for most was in the billions and in my case the chance of meeting a duplicate of another in the normal course of my life was nearly impossible.

Intrigued and because the use of Michael by New Jerusalem had already mapped out the DNA of each individual, and would continue to do so, I gained access to Michael's DNA database and began searching for perfect matches. It took me ten years because of the small number of survivors left by the war, but I finally found a match. Terra and Felicity."

Mr. Page during his conversation, began slouching a bit and catching himself sat upright again. "Terra was ninety-three and Felicity had just been born. So given the advanced age of Mrs. Terra, I convinced my supervisors to allow me to travel to her hometown with Mr. Dulant; so that we could map her brain and I could double check the DNA data myself. I confirmed that the DNA was indeed the same. This was an obvious flaw in Michael's design.

A special tag for each person's information and some alterations in Michael's log keeping was all that was needed to solve the logistical problem, but my curiosity compelled me to continue. Because of my discovery, New Jerusalem was willing to let me peruse the matter in any way I saw fit. With unlimited resources and all my time, the data I began finding was amazing."

He stared out of one of the windows to the tangle of hardware outside our room. "I gathered the best psychologists we had and began pouring over Terra's vocal and visual data. It took us countless hours and hundreds of personnel, but we were able to map out Terra's psychology in the term of a year. Time was of the essence. Next, after scouring our nation, we put Felicity with parents that most closely resembled, in as much as possible, Terra's parents. We provided the house and financing so that it would also be comparable to Terra's upbringing. Over a course of twenty years we watched over this family; implementing Terra's major life hurdles when it was appropriate for Felicity's life."

For the first time in Mr. Page's explanation, he showed an expression and slightly smiled. "Do you know what we found? Terra and Felicity were the same person. Felicity reacted the same as Terra when Terra's problems were presented in her life. I died and this research continued until the death of Felicity, who at the age of ninety-three had an identical brain to Terra.

The research continued for another generation without much progress beyond what we had already established. I was revived genetically and re-taught using the notes and literature I had accumulated in my past life. Ironically, the research I pioneered was now being used on me and had become the basis that made my resurrection sensible. I continued my work. But instead of focusing on perfect matches I began experimenting with similar matches and without going into detail, I found that matches with a high percentage of similarity didn't always yield, mentally, the same person. Just as true, low percentages sometimes brought up exact psychological matches. Using the hundred percent DNA match as a control, I consistently found that my original research proved to be true for all subjects.

This was when Mr. Dulant's specialties were needed." Mr. Page made a motion towards Mr. Dulant with an up-facing hand as if he were passing him some tangible object."

Mr. Dulant, who had been slouching and yawning during Mr. Page's explanation, sat up. "Thank you Mr. Page. Well, this is where, because of Mr. Page's good grace, and because of my work with the reconfiguration of Michael, that I was revived as well and taught using my research. Thanks to Mr. Page's work it was clear that a perfect matching DNA sequence wasn't needed to produce the same person. Given that a person is defined in this case by their mental characteristics rather than physical, it was also clear that the missing link we needed to find was one between DNA and the function of the brain."

Mr. Dulant faced towards Mr. Page with his half smile on his face. "So number two me worked with number three Mr. Page to find that connection." This simplification of their reincarnations clearly bothered Mr. Page.

"We took Mr. Page's data from subjects with percentages of DNA that yielded the same person along with my research on the human brain and began narrowing down what codons might be responsible for the duplication of these people. This took generation after generation of continuous research with a team of scientists until we were able to narrow down the codons by comparing subjects and using the process of elimination." He gave an expression of exhaustion. "We then tested and retested our theory until we were sure we had come up with a new, much smaller, pool of codons for mankind that if found and analyzed in a person, represented a unique individual. You know these as Adam and Eve."

Mr. Dulant paused and faced Mr. Page. Mr. Page then continued, "Our research proved what my first findings hinted to: mankind was immortal because of recurring sets of DNA and with the plotting of the Adam and Eve codons in people, mankind's true number of individuals was greatly reduced. With this, our comprehension of who we were was vastly different. We could now point out several people and accurately say these are the same person."

Chapter 4

We had been taught of our immortality, but we hadn't been told the basis behind it; only that it was cyclical. "How many unique individuals are there Sir?"

Mr. Dulant slouched again in his previous manner. Mr. Page, as if ignoring Mr. Dulant, turned more towards my direction. "There were about nine billion humans on this earth before the Nuclear War. We know this through the data that we inherited. Through our calculations we found that regardless of this number, only two hundred and forty three thousand and three hundred and fifty was the number of true individuals. That number remained unchanged until the appearance of the Levite."

Page's round face lit up with his last sentence, then slowly settled. "But, later our research brought up a deleterious question: If we are immortal, what of heaven? What of religion? ...What of God? We had unwittingly stumbled upon our society's destruction. If everyone is immortal and regardless of what they do, their life on this earth is assured through the cycle of life and death, then what is the point of anything?

We tried to delay the inevitable as long as possible, but our research was eventually discovered by the masses. In a matter of years murders, assaults, theft and crime in general increased ten fold. We had the tools and data to identify each perpetrator, but not the manpower to bring them to justice. Complete chaos had taken over."

Again, a slight smile crept across Mr. Page's face betraying his normal demeanor. "It was then that I presented myself to the tattered remains of New Jerusalem's government and purposed to create a God here on earth to give the people something to follow. With no other choice and every conventional resource exhausted they agreed. Miss. Debora, Mr. Dulant and I gathered a team and after three years of research and the constant threat of a governmental collapse we created the first version of the Levite."

I could feel my pulse begin to race, my eyes widened and I managed to gasp, "You created the Levite?!"

Mr. Page unaffected by my reaction, turned his right palm upward and in a tone of frustration said, "Humanity created the Levite. Though the Levite is my greatest pride and joy, his creation was a possibility since the discovery of Adam and Eve. I was afraid of what would transpire if we would make such a being, but the childish reaction by the population forced our hand. Our government was at the edge of collapse; the number of moral people was dwindling. We didn't have the time or any other choice. Hoping to have found the answer and that he would be good, we made the Levite out of the Adam and Eve DNA of the people that were still law abiding and taught him everything we knew. The Levite poured over our data base and with the use of Michael, in a matter of months (which would have taken us decades), unleashed several Adam and Eve DNA specific viruses and wiped out every criminal from the face of the earth."

Mr. Dulant's gaze slowly focused in my direction and in an uneasy manner sat up straight. Mr. Page simply continued. "A primal fear collectively shot through all humanity that day. The Levite had created Michael's second half and in turn had eradicated more than two thirds of the unique individuals in our population. The Levite gave us peace again. He reinterpreted The Bible. He separated those with the mark of Cane from the Elect. He gave us a heaven to strive for and brought back death to our world."

With these last words Mr. Page stood up, "I believe the best thing to do now is to take a tour of Michael."

Chapter 5

I felt as if my head was spinning. The Levite had been created by humans? And then the Levite in turn "eradicates" more than two thirds of them. None of this made sense.

Plainly seeing my frustration, Mr. Page simply reiterated what he had told me in the past. "None of this will make too much sense to you until you speak to the Levite."

We walked out of our quiet niche and into the chaotic symphony of the machines of Michael.

Mr. Page began his tour by pointing in the direction of the machinery, "As you know, those that have been deemed unworthy of living among us are those with the mark of Cane," he paused and looked at me, at which I nodded my head in confirmation. "Well the viruses that are made to keep them from living among us are made here in this section of Michael. Of course if the viruses were made to simply attack DNA our perpetrators would just come back as different people; so these viruses are made to attack Adam and Eve DNA so that any iteration of them will be wiped out."

We continued walking to a section filled with tubes that all fed into large pipes. "The viruses are pumped from here into the atmosphere in which other facilities spaced around the world then make the same commodity. Only this facility produces new viruses." Mr. Page's demeanor about the whole situation seemed detached and cold. "In the beginning the Levite used humans as a source to spread the viruses, but now because of our smaller numbers it was changed to just airborne." Mr. Page paused near the large pipes. "Most viruses now are made to prevent the development of fetuses, but every now and then some are released to target a grown person." He continued walking.

We arrived at where all the facilities wires seemed to converge. Mr. Page stopped, "This is where Michael receives the Levite's information. Only the Levite has this clearance and only he creates the viruses." I stared at it for a moment, a mindless automaton; the hilt of the sword.

We began once again and arrived at a large space with thousands of servers. Mr. Page stopped at the entrance and with a wave of his hand, began, "This is an archive which contains the data Michael has collected from the life of everyone that has lived and will ever live. The last place where those with the mark of Cane abode with the elect."

Mr. Dulant with a sort of somber appearance, walked over to a server and patting it as if it were a child stated. "Here's me... As many times as I have seen it I can't get used to it. My analogue" He bent down a bit concentrating on some lights as if he were staring at it's eyes.

Though this time it was obvious that Mr. Dulant had no ulterior motives for his comments, Mr. Page was frustrated just the same.

"Lets continue." said Mr. Page looking in my direction.

We headed to a separate room. It was just as large and equally furnished. "Here we have a piece of God," said Mr. Page with great pride. "It is mankind's accumulative knowledge, all the truths we have reaped from this world. We all are honored with a fraction of it but only the Levite has the ability to truly appreciate it as a whole." Mr. Page exhaled with an expression of contentment on his face.

The tour being over we headed back to the vehicle and said our goodbyes to Mr. Dulant, an act that was done more heartily by Mr. Page than he had his salutation.

It had become dark outside which gave our ride back a sort of tranquility as we stared at the lights of our destination peering over the horizon.

"Was the Levite among the servers we saw today Mr. Page?" I asked. He had sat down as he looked at the lights.

"No, the Levite has no record. Towards the end of his lifetime he makes another in his image, a clone, and then entails a plan for his upbringing. From his birth he is directly and indirectly taught and inspected by the Levite until the time comes for him to meet God." Mr. Page calmly stared at the lights during his whole explanation.

I also sat down; it didn't seem appropriate to press the subject. I turned around and looked at the stars that had consoled me in the past, in what seemed a lifetime ago.

Chapter 6

My morning was a reenactment of yesterdays. Once I had finished preparing, Mr. Page who seemed in unusual high spirits gave me the good news. "Today you will see the Levite and the Elect."

This excited me greatly. Finally, definitive answers to the questions that had been brought up these past days. We began walking towards the Levites room, when we arrived Mr. Page stepped aside and once again I was left to push the crimson doors open.

Inside was the Levite sitting behind his large desk. He was no longer busily distracted, but was waiting for me. I walked in and took a seat as the door was closed behind me.

The Levite stood, his height was staggering, something that his desk had previously concealed. "I'll start with the basis of our religion. You are familiar with the story of Adam and Eve in Genesis?" I was watching him move about. Without looking at me for a confirmation to his question, he just continued. "It was a common conception that this was the beginning of mankind's woes. A curse from God, the original sin. Adam and Eve cast out from the garden of Eden for their transgression." He stood still for a moment, his blank yellow eyes looking into mine. "Do you know what it really was?" He just continued as before. "A blessing from God.

He had given humanity the choice of whether to live in content with what they had or to be as he was, to be Gods. Mankind chose to eat the fruit of good and evil. They chose to take the path of understanding, of knowledge and power. And God with his eternal mercy set the path to their desire before them. Necessity is the mother of all invention, so god gave them need. Death, hunger, fear, the elements; are all magnificent motivators for mankind's evolution into something better. Because of God's grace, humanity has continued reaping and eating from the same forbidden fruit from this world since their exile. It was in my first life that I was acquainted with God and came to this realization. This whole world is cyclical composition and decomposition over and over again. However, I found that there was an exception... knowledge." He began walking again, "Knowledge is the exception but only in a special set of circumstances. It has to be recorded and carried on so it doesn't fall into the same destructive and constructive cycle. In other words, so that people don't continuously keep reinventing the wheel. You see they've always had the same teacher. The same available lessons and pupils, so there wouldn't be any progress unless they had a collective recollection of where they left off. Congruently, a continuous society becomes a necessity to assure the constant survival of knowledge."

He let out a slight laugh. "This is another gift from God. Mankind has an inborn desire and need to build societies. Look at every major religion that has come up through their history. All of them have the same foundation: rules and regulations that make their society possible. Their religion's purpose was more practical even though they praised and followed it as a salvation for the after life. But what power does Earthly restrictions have on the development of life in another world? Do you really think that a God, or Gods put mankind on this earth to merely see if they can follow commands? No. I saw God the day I absorbed humanities knowledge. God is truth. That is why I made the religion and the society you see today; that is why I made you. You and I are the same person."

I almost felt my heart stop, but before I could say anything, without looking at me, he lifted his finger and continued talking.

"If God is truth and the only thing on this Earth that mankind can have that is eternal is accumulative knowledge, then their path to heaven and God is clear. Heaven will be built by them on Earth, through knowledge, with God. That is why we wiped out two thirds of humanity and have continued to choose the Elect. Those who are not contributing to mankind's heaven are deemed parasites and as such, their Adam and Eve genome is identified as the mark of Cane and are wiped out. The Elect are those that work hard, that contribute, that prove themselves worthy of living in heaven forever because they have built themselves a place in it."

He sat down behind his desk. "We were not the God that Page had envisioned but his Preacher, mankind's shepherd. We, on that day, put humanity on their rightful path and have continued to do so using Michael.

When a person is born their Adam and Eve genome is identified and their mental and physical potential is measured. After, they are placed in a position that best suites their gifts; by us. Following this, they are left to do as they please and after their death we evaluate their life to see if they have lived up to their potential and whether or not they have contributed to societies progression. We then decide if they will be allowed to reincarnate or be marked for termination. With an exception, if a person commits a heinous crime such as murder or assault they are immediately evaluated. Then, depending on the circumstances, they are either marked or given another chance."

He leaned forward and tapped both his index and middle finger on his desk. "You see, all these rules that have made societies possible and have been innate in mankind's psyche since the beginning now have a greater purpose. Instead of simply appeasing some taxing God these rules, if followed, guarantee a well-structured society and the progression of knowledge. In other words, it guarantees that humanity takes a step closer to their heaven and to a manifestation of God here on earth.

It is all a gift... when humanity ate of the fruit of knowledge of good and evil. They became defined by it. It is in knowing what good and evil is that then makes a person, good or evil. This is God's gift of choice. Animals and Angels cannot be either since they don't know what each is. They are only what they are... they have no choice. But there is something beyond good, there is perfection."

He sat back again. "God is truth, but the true God is absolute truth, God is perfection. Something humanity hasn't achieved yet. The God I saw that day and have continued to see isn't his full form. Knowledge in this world is finite, and since they are immortal they will one day, with work and direction, find it all. On that day their true God will be revealed and with him not only will they build their own heaven but will become gods themselves, because they will know what God knows."

He paused and looked in my direction for a moment. "We are Levites, and because God is our only inheritance we have only what immortal humanity has given us. We were created with the Adam and Eve DNA of the Elect. Our DNA is not cyclical like theirs. We have only one lifetime and with it only one purpose: to direct humanity to their heaven to the best of our abilities."

Chapter 7

"Why was I made by you Sir and not Mr. Page?" It was the first question that had surfaced to mind.

"Page only made our first incarnation; afterwards it has always been the current Levite that makes the next. The reason why is simple, our abilities are beyond that of a human and because of it we are more qualified for the task."

"Well Sir, and by this I mean no offense, is it not easier for us to do all the science and technological advances rather than managing humanity?" My voice shook a bit.

"Yes, if the only goal was to create a heaven on earth. Except there is a second question that we need to answer. Who is worthy of entering heaven? In past religions it was believed a person was dealt certain attributes in life and was then judged by their god or divine entity. They now know that people live through several lifetimes with several inherent advantages and disadvantages in which they are then judged by us, as a whole.

It is one of our jobs to decide who is good and who is bad by the actions they have chosen in their lifetimes. By using Michael and our database, we can accurately do that. Rather than unfairly condemning a person who has had nothing but hardships in their life as bad and then exalting another who has had a charmed life, we are judging people at their core by watching them in all scenarios and then deciding whether they are good or evil. We do this because a heaven would not be self-sustainable if evil people were allowed to enter.

He stood up. "It will be more appropriate if I show you the answers to the next questions you might have, instead of answering them here. Go to Page and get ready, your going to meet the Elect this afternoon."

I pushed open the doors. I found Mr. Page waiting for me in his usual manner. "This way Sir. We have to get you ready." I could see his high spirits were still with him.

"Where are we going now sir?" I was confused as to our next destination since we had gone beyond the maze of rooms.

Mr. Page, now going at a fast pace, answered without looking back. "There is a stage in the back of this building that opens to a spectacular view of the city. There will be a room behind it where you will get ready for the Levite's sermon. It will be given before a celebration."

"His sermon?" I couldn't help but be surprised.

"Yes." We had arrived at the room Mr. Page had mentioned and as he turned around, I was astonished. A large smile ran across Mr. Page's round face. Given his normal demeanor it seemed almost unnatural, almost as if it had been pasted on. "Ah, this will be a real treat." he grinned. "I almost envy you. To see it for the first time." He paused with his smile growing larger and looked at his watch.

Suddenly, I felt the whole place shake. Startled, I looked at Mr. Page who was facing up, still smiling with his eyes closed. He exhaled, "It's starting... your clothes are in this room, get ready and then we'll go meet the Levite before he begins."

I went in and could feel that the place was shaking along with a rhythm. My clothes looked the same as what everyone and I had always worn, except they were green. I put them on and followed Mr. Page. As we began to walk further, the thumps that were shaking the building got louder until I could feel them vibrating through me. We arrived at a door and Mr. Page, arriving to it, simply stepped aside. Being already familiar with this gesture, I stepped forward and opened the door.

Behind it was the Levite. He had on an ephod of the same color as my clothes with a golden breastplate over it. It had the same twelve stones I had seen on the Levite's red door. He turned to me and picked up two small flat stones with markings on them.

He smiled and put them in a pocket on his ephod. "Urim and Thummim, good and evil." He then walked up to an opposing door from where

I had come in. The door was in the direction of the continuous beating; that now synced and took on the rhythm of a heart.

The Levite signaled me to get closer with his hand, and with another smile opened the door.

We walked down a corridor, our footsteps being drowned by the beating. I could see bright lights hitting the wall where it ended. When we walked out I almost fell back. An ocean of people. They received us with a deafening cheer. I squinted my eyes and found in front of the multitude Mr. Page, Miss. Debora and Mr. Dulant. All three had seats in front, but Mr. Dulant had left his to yell among the crowd. The Levite signaled me to take a seat and walked to the center of the stage. The crowd, still stomping their rhythm, came to an almost hysterical pitch.

The Levite lifted his right hand towards the crowd. "'So that thou incline thine ear unto wisdom, and apply thine heart to understanding.'"[1] He brought both hands into fists in front of his chest and yelled, "'Yea, if thou criest after knowledge, and liftest up thy voice for understanding. If thou seekest her as silver, and searchest for her as for hid treasures.'"[1] Walking he pointed towards the mass of people. "'Then shalt thou understand the fear of the LORD, and find the knowledge of God.'"[1]

This was received with a massive cheer by the Elect, which paled their previous effort.

The Levite waited until their cry died down. "We are so close." He pointed in my direction. "We are at the door." He paused and looked at the crowd. "Who can slow us? Who can hinder us? Who can stop us now?! This last question thundered out in a yell.

Again the crowd let out a consuming shout. He continued, "Because of you, because of all of you! This is your inheritance!" He thrust his hand down pointing at the ground." And it's here around you; all you have to do is take it. "'Ask, and it shall be given you; seek, and ye shall find; knock, and it shall be opened unto you.'"2 He began pacing. "'For every one that asketh receiveth; and he that seeketh findeth; and to him that knocketh it shall be opened.'"2

He stood still and looked at the ocean that stood in front of him. "Who can stop us?... No one! Your path is the same as it has always been; your path is in front of you. 'No man, having put his hand to the plough, and looking back, is fit for the kingdom of God!'"3

"We are almost there. You only need to take another step, to progress, to knock, to ask, to search! We have almost found our true God, he is almost visible, he is almost tangible. What's left is around you. All you need to do is dig him up from the earth; find this silver, uncover what's left of the treasure.

I looked at the crowd: thousands upon thousands of faces shouting, weeping. I could feel their stomping heart beat pulsing through me. Shaking my body to their rhythm and the Levite shouting, gesturing, conducting. Amazing, I thought, the body and mind.

The Levite began again in a calmer voice, "You have only to do your part. You are the Elect. 'A good tree cannot bring forth evil fruit, neither can a corrupt tree bring forth good fruit.'4 Our destination is inevitable, 'For there is nothing covered, that shall not be revealed; neither hid, that shall not be known.'5 You only need to remember to walk"

"I hope that by the next time I stand here in front of you." He directed his hand towards me. "That we would have already reached our destination together. 'The LORD by wisdom hath founded the earth; by understanding hath he established the heavens.'6 We need only find it."

The Elect's shouts grew to a peak and with it the Levite began to walk back down the corridor and I followed behind him. The festival would now start.

When we arrived at the room where I had seen the Levite, I saw that Mr. Page was at the door. He looked as if he had been crying.

The Levite gestured toward Mr. Page. "Page will take you back to your room. Tomorrow you will take your first step... This flock is your only inheritance, that and the fact that you will be the first to truly see God."

As I looked back my eyes met the Levites. After a brief moment I turned around and followed Mr. Page back to my room.

I lied down to sleep, but I couldn't, I felt ecstatic. The sermon was amazing; I felt purpose for the first time. I laid there for what felt like an eternity, until I began to doze off to the sound of my own heartbeat.

Chapter 8

I was walking, stumbling, when I opened my eyes. I was amongst the Elect in the city. Everyone was moving up and down to the command of their day's chores. As I looked around I noticed that the whole city was as I had seen it before, except it was built completely out of wood. No one was noticing me. After some walking, I saw a vulture circling in the sky off in the distance towards the center of our city. I began to move in its direction and found a huge thick garden that hadn't been there before. I looked around and it seemed as no one else saw it. I pushed aside some branches and went in.

The inside was beautiful; a wide variety of trees, plants, and creatures. I looked around as I walked through the thicket: Panthera Leo, Olea europaea, Apis Mellifera… suddenly I saw that I wasn't alone. Sitting on a large tree trunk below a hole in the canopy, below the circling vulture, was the Levite. I could recognize his lanky, long figure. He was leaning forward looking attentively at something in his hand.

I walked up to him and found that he had one of the Urim and Thummim stones in his hand and was shuffling it through his fingers; much the same as he had done with his pen when I first met him.

I sat next to him and after a moment of watching him continue, I asked, "Why is it that no one else sees this place Sir?"

His yellow eyes concentrated on manipulating the stone. He let out a scoff of a laugh, "They don't recognize it."

"Why do we Sir?" I began to feel uneasy.

With his face still facing the stone he looked towards me from the corner of his eye. "'The people that walked in darkness have seen a great light: they that dwell in the land of the shadow of death, upon them hath the light shined.'"7

I woke up gasping for air. I was drenched in sweat and my heart was racing. Chill after chill ran through my spine. I threw off my sheets and sat up, my breath keeping pace with my heart. I wiped the sweat from my face and walked up to the window. Slowly my breathing began to return to normal and as I watched over the city lights, a feeling of dread came over me.

When I awoke the next day I tried to shrug off my dream. I began to prepare for the day, but as I crossed over to the shower I noticed that Mr. Page wasn't waiting for me in the hall. Instead I found the Levite in his place.

Startled I paused and stared at him, "Good day Sir."

"Good day to you." he seemed amused by my reaction.

"And Mr..."

"Page?" he had finished my question. "Yes, he's waiting for us in another room, in another building, west from this one." His voice was a slow draw.

I looked in his direction for another moment. "Excuse me Sir." I went in and got ready. When I came out, the Levite began walking in the direction he had mentioned.

"Why...?"

"Why am I here and not Page." The Levite said it more as a statement than a question. "What you will see next is our work and it only seemed appropriate that I would be the one to introduce you to it." He began walking down some stairs that split off to the right of the hall. "Not only is Page there but so is Dulant and Debora." He added with a smile.

I was still curious but I also felt uneasy.

The building we entered seemed to be a sort of hospital. There were gurneys, IVs, and monitors in every room; but no patients.

We came to a room that seemed a bit larger than the others. Inside were Mr. Page, Miss. Debora and Mr. Dulant waiting each in a seat near a large bed with monitors, blue sheets, and robotic arms that hovered over it from the ceiling.

My heart began to race. "Good day." Regardless of my fear, etiquette had become a reflex. All three stood up and returned the greeting.

The Levite sat down and picked up from a steel tray, what seemed like a grain of rice.

"This is what I wanted to show you. This, and you is what I have been working on for the better part of my life." He smiled as he raised it to get a better view of it with the room's light.

"Questions, young man, questions direct a conversation. Hardships, problems are the questions of life. With this you will find out whether you are worthy of continuing or not." He gave me a large smile. "Call me a narcissist but I think you have nothing to worry about."

My eyes were focused on the granule the Levite held. "What is it Sir?"

The Levite smiled once again. "The Tabernacle of God." His smile grew to show his teeth. "You see this makes everything obsolete. The whole building in which you met Miss. Debora was devoted for the purpose of teaching Levites. That huge maze is no longer necessary because of this. The constant monitoring of Michael, which I would then have to scour through its data to judge our citizens, is no longer required. Having to pour through mankind's archives of knowledge to continuously monitor and direct their progress will also now be archaic; because of this," he pointed at me with the grain he had between his fingers. "Because of you."

"This Tabernacle, once implanted into your brain, will work like Michael in reverse. You will receive all the auditory and visual information of the elect, along with all the accumulative knowledge and progress in their data banks. Building such a devise wasn't so difficult. Making you was the real challenge. It is both conceit full and humbling to say, but you are as far from me as I was from Page the day I was created." The Levite sat back in his seat and set down his creation. "I made you with the capacity of taking in this massive amount of information and still be able to retain it. The question you will confront today is, whether or not, you will be able to retain yourself."

Mr. Dulant gave me an apron to wear as he and the Levite went into another room. Miss. Debora looked over the robotic arms and then moved to an adjacent room full of monitors along with Mr. Page. Mr. Dulant, and the Levite both came out wearing surgical gear.

Mr. Dulant bent forward, his face covered by a mask. "Don't worry, this whole building was made for this day. I've already done something similar to this one hundred and ten times?" His eyes squinted tighter as he formed a question towards the end of his sentence. "One hundred and twelve? Well anyways I can't really count the first ones." I began to feel more anxious. "The important thing is that I have implanted the Michael device into enough people after their infant stage to know what I'm doing."

Before I could state my concerns he put a surgical gas mask over my mouth and nose.

Chapter 9

I found myself walking among the Elect once again. Instinctively, I looked in the direction where I had seen the circling vulture and found it as before, hovering, waiting. I decided to continue watching the Elect and because of curiosity, to see what made up their day.

Everyone was silently walking up and down the streets, in and out of the wooden buildings. Through no important reason I chose an older gentleman to follow. He had caught my eye because of his brisk pace.

I thought humorously, "Here's a man that knows what's, what. Important places to go and things to do." I chuckled a bit as I went into a slight jog in order to catch up to him. It was also no coincidence that this man happened to be heading in the opposite direction of the circling vulture.

I followed him through a few streets. He was fumbling through some papers and notes he had pressed up to his chest with his left arm. His eyes would dart from some sentence or note he currently had in his right hand to the route he was taking. Sporadically he would raise his hand along with whatever parchment he was currently scanning, in a greeting to a passer by.

We arrived to what seemed his place of work. He dropped his papers with no great care on his desk and threw both his coat and hat on a hat tree with impressive precision. I watched the hat tree wobble then center itself.

He began shuffling through the papers and after finding what he had been looking for, he walked into an adjacent room where two of his colleagues were imputing something into their computers. He showed it to them, I couldn't hear what they were saying, it seemed like a sort of epiphany he had ran across and was explaining it to them. I watched, trying to guess what they were saying. I saw that they had typed something into their computer, but when I looked at the monitor I found nothing. It was the same with the note the man had in his hand; to me it was completely blank.

I sat on the floor and watched them. I tried to form the words of their conversation without any real conclusion. Though, as I watched, suddenly, I heard the voice of one the colleagues. "How did you come up with this?"

The man with the note answered in an exuberant voice. "I was sitting at home breaking my head over it when I noticed the sequence of colors in the tabs of my notes. It isn't an exact link to our problem, but it got me thinking to the sequence of frequencies we were looking into that we discarded as a dead end. I looked over our notes and found that if we paired the data we have gotten so far from our current experiments we would..."

"What's the PH in the solution?" Another voice interrupted. I looked around startled but found no one else. "Remember you want it to be a PH of two before you heat it."

I looked around again confused. Then suddenly, I saw what was written on the monitor of one of the computers, but not through my point of view. It looked as if I was looking at it through the eyes of one of the colleagues.

My mind started to race. I began hearing pieces of conversations that then turned into segments of words. My mind was overwhelmed, flashes of people, objects, animals, and a torrent of other things passed through my sight. I closed them and cupped my ears but still they rushed in. "What is happening?" I mouthed the words but heard nothing. I found it hard to concentrate. My mind kept switching from this mass of sights and sounds, to trying to comprehend what was going on. Slowly, I felt my mind slipping. I began losing my grasp; it was being washed away into the huge body of information I was receiving.

Chapter 10

"We're losing him Sir, his mind isn't coming up on the monitors." Debora's voice came from the speakerphone.

I pushed the button on the intercom, "Yes, this is where it starts."

"Well, the implantation of the Tabernacle went as it should have, Sir. His brain function though, is all over the place." Dulant stooped over a monitor next to Jacob. "Guess it's a matter of waiting now."

"Yes the next step is up to him." I watched Jacob as he blankly stared at the ceiling. His eyes dilated, dashing around in every direction, with his lips open, slightly mouthing the syllables of incomplete words.

I thought, "What a privilege." If only I could take the same journey you are. Though, I would have died the instant I would have received the first rush of information. You surviving as long as you have, alone, shows the chasm between us. A weary smile came to my face as a thought came to mind. "No man that hath a blemish of the seed of Aaron the priest shall come nigh to offer the offerings of the LORD made by fire: he hath a blemish; he shall not come nigh to offer the bread of his God."8

"We'll wait seven days to let his mind get acclimated before we transfer mankind's accumulative knowledge to the Tabernacle. After that, we'll begin trying to bring him back." I changed out of scrubs and left Jacob to the care of Dulant, Debora, and Page.

I walked to my room and clenched my fists, pride and jealousy overwhelmed me. "We are at the door and you Jacob will open it." I looked around at my notes, monitors, and general work that had consumed my life. "I'm almost at my wicks end. This has been my purpose since the beginning and now its onset has marked my death."

I sat down, my eyes still focused on my work. Their stretched out shadows forming silhouettes on the wall. I rubbed my hand over my head and exhaled my inevitable axiom: "The sun rises in the east and sets in the west."

I returned to Jacob on the appointed day and found his body hooked to IVs and feeding tubes. "How is he doing?"

It was Page who answered. "He's doing better Sir. His mind has briefly showed up on our instruments."

"Good, now give him the rest of the information." I watched Jacob as his eyes dilated and then went back to their previous size. I couldn't help but smile. "How's his brain function Dulant?"

Dulant walked over to the monitor. "It fluctuated immensely Sir, but it has gone back to normal. He certainly took this information much better."

"We'll wait and use flash cards at night when the information he will be receiving will diminish and only come in sporadically through the Elect's REM sleep."

"Flash cards Sir?" Dulant's tone seemed to second-guess my low-tech approach.

I looked over at him and immediately saw he had realized his mistake. "Yes."

"Sorry, Sir."

I walked up to him and patted his shoulder. "It doesn't need to be complicated."

We sat down and waited for nightfall. I watched Jacob spasm, along with peaks of information on the monitors confirming his mental presence.

Everyone watched the monitors as the clock struck the hour of curfew. After a few more hours, Jacob's mind began coming in stronger.

Debora looked over the instruments to make sure all the readings were coming in accurately, while Dulant read them. Dulant moved from monitor to monitor making comparisons to the notes he took in the beginning of the procedure.

"It seems this is as good as it gets, Sir. Unless you want to wait for any restless body that might still be about." Dulant spoke as he flipped over his notes again and began rechecking the information.

"No, I'm sure this will be good enough. I'm going to have to ask you and Debora to go into the room with Page and relate the resulting information from there." I took a seat in front of Jacob with the flashcards in hand.

Dulant straggled behind. "May I ask you something, Sir?"

I looked back from my seat. "Yes."

Debora paused at the door and Dulant took a step forward. "How will flash cards help bring back his mind, Sir? And what's on them?"

I put the flash cards face down on the metal tray and turned the seat around. "When someone is presented with a word or small group of words that are legible and familiar, they will automatically read it; regardless if they want to or not. On these cards are words that will only be recognizable and understood by him because of the knowledge he has absorbed. I know them as well of course, but since I don't have Michael implanted in me, I am not transferring this data through to him until I show him the cards. The important thing is, that when he receives these words he is receiving them in his own voice, sort to say, so that he can then recognize himself. It is also important that none of you see these words so that the information doesn't come in through you and he simply recognizes another person among many that are already in his mind.

Debora and Dulant both smiled, "Thank you Sir," and went into the room. I turned my seat again and picked up the cards.

Trames. Semita. Limes. Callis. Via. Iter. Itiner. Trames. Semita. Limes. Callis. Via. Iter. Itiner. Trames. Semita. Limes. Callis. Via. Iter. Itiner.

"His mind is almost completely coming through, Sir." Dulant's voice was heard out of the speaker.

Suddenly, Jacob's eye's focused. In a panic he pulled out his feeding tube and IVs. His eyes began to dilate again. He punched the corner of the chairs arm; sending out a cry along with the sound of bones breaking. Jacob's mind seemed to focus once again; he held his head in his hands and bent forward. After a moment, he ran out of the room.

Page came running out but I stopped him. "There's nothing we can help him in now. I'm sure he'll find a way."

Chapter 11

My hand was throbbing. I concentrated on the pain. I could barely keep my thoughts straight but managed to find my way out of the building. I navigated the streets by moonlight, stopping periodically to squeeze my broken hand for clarity.

"I have to get to the forest before daytime or else I'll lose myself again before I make it." I was gasping for air and sweating profusely; the concentration it took to simply say those words was immense. I began running, watching the horizon for any sign of the sun; getting there felt like an eternity. When I finally arrived I didn't pause but continued at the same pace deeper into the wilderness.

As I ran I could feel my connection to my body begin to sever. At moments my limbs felt none existent, my left leg at mid stride went limp causing me to fall. On the ground, I managed to turn over and form a fist with my shattered hand; I stood up and began again.

The sounds and sights started coming in stronger and stronger. I looked up at my stars and watched the sunlight dissolve them as I blacked out.

I found myself walking in an empty space. "Am I dead?" I could no longer hear and see the Elect. I began walking but found quickly that there wasn't any progress to be made. There wasn't any way to establish direction or headway. I sat down. I felt exhausted mentally and physically.

"Did I die of thirst?" I looked down at my crossed legs and then felt a breeze. I took a deep breath and stood up. I put my hand out in front of me and felt the air pass between my fingers. I began walking in its direction.

I found another person walking toward me. It looked as if I were walking into my own reflection. He was the same size and body shape as me, but when I got close enough I found that he had no face.

I took a step back, as did he.

His face was a blur of movement; I couldn't stop staring. I began to recognize faces of the Elect. Their faces were shifting at an incredible speed, from one to another, in front of this person's head.

"Do you know who I am?" His voice resounded and seemed to be made up of thousands of others.

"The Elect?" I began to feel an incredible pressure come over my body.

"Yes and no. I am them, and I am you." He continued to mimic my movements.

Weariness came over my body again. I sat down and my companion mirrored me.

"So... Where am I?... Did I die?"

"No, but you are about to." His voice didn't seem to come from the body that sat in front of me, but instead, felt as if it was being projected from all around.

I sat there watching him watch me. I stared into the haze that was his face. I felt more and more fatigued. My body felt as if it was made of lead. I could hear my breath slow down and become heavier.

"Our path is one without end. The human body is nothing but an anchor and this world is only a mirror... Our god is appetite. God's true image is not of this world. We can recognize him only through self-reflection. God is freedom from our anchor."

"Humanities greatest gift is not the ability to change this world, it is the ability to change themselves."

He stood up as I called on the last ounces of strength to do the same. He outstretched his arm towards me and I stretched mine towards him. Our hands touched and we walked into each other.

I awoke in a bed; in what seemed like the same building level in which the Tabernacle was implanted in me.

I moved my head to the side a bit. I felt exhausted. I could feel heat coming off part of my face where the sun had burned me. My arms had insect bites all across them. I lifted my hand in front of my face; I had lost an incredible amount of weight.

I lay there and watched the ceiling. What a curious feeling. I know what everyone is doing at this moment. I know the faces and names of every person on earth and because of the information I'm receiving, with time, I will become more familiar with them than anyone they know. It isn't a burden or relentless torrent anymore. My thoughts and the Elect are now completely separated. It feels more like an inborn knowledge that I can reference at any time.

I heard footsteps, then saw the Levite and Mr. Page stand over me. Mr. Page smiled. "You were out there for weeks. When we retrieved you we were barely able to resuscitate you, Sir." I could see the joy in his face.

"We knew where you were because of the Tabernacle." The Levite stood up straight. "I understood what you were trying to do. You were trying to find yourself mentally by bringing your body to the point of death. So that your primal instinct of survival would consume whatever was going through your mind. You could then concentrate on the physical aspects of dying; unique to your body." The Levite sat down in a chair next to me. "The delicate part was when to go out and retrieve you, that is, before you died. We were receiving your mental and health statistics, but it still wasn't easy. You came dangerously close to dying before your mental data showed you had achieved a separation from the Elect." He looked over at Mr. Page. "We were thinking of retrieving you before this point, but I'm glad we stuck it out." He gave me a large smile and a pat on my arm. "Well done."

Mr. Page was still leaning forward. "Out of curiosity Sir, did you see anything?"

"Yes." My voice was hoarse and I could feel blisters on my lips from exposure. "I saw a reflective surface that seemed to separate life and death. There was no distinction between both... until I crossed over." As I spoke I became lost in thought. I remembered the reflection I had seen of myself, and what it had told me. I felt uneasy.

The room was quiet; both the Levite and Mr. Page were staring at me. I looked over at the Levite, "I need to speak to you Sir, as soon as you have a chance.

The Levite acknowledged my request with a nod. "But first I want you to fully recuperate, then we will have plenty of time to talk." The Levite walked out the room with Mr. Page behind him.

I don't know what the Levite did beyond Mr. Page's sight, but Mr. Page, walked into my room and in a very gleeful manner began looking it over, fluffing my pillows, dusting, (even though there wasn't any dust), and in general, preparing it for my return. It warmed my heart to watch through his eyes the generosity and love he had for me. It was almost as if he saw the Levite and I as his sons; in many ways we are.

I went back to watching the ceiling. I couldn't shake the feeling of anxiety I had. "We are on the wrong path."

Chapter 12

It took me a few weeks to recover during which that same thought persisted. It was in the last day of the second week the Levite summoned me to his room, due to my request.

I entered and found him looking over some papers on his desk. When he saw me he put down his pen and sat down while gesturing me to do the same.

He looked me in the eyes. "What you told Page and I about your dream wasn't everything you saw, was it?"

"No Sir. I saw a revelation when I was dying, and... " I hesitated. "Because of it I believe we are on the wrong path."

"On the wrong path?" He smiled as he said it. "Then illuminate me. What is the right path?" He had a sarcastic tone.

"You have detailed and built a path for a perfect world, but not a perfect people. Humanity was made in Gods image, and the path to perfection lies in their soul, their psychology, not on this world. God is perfection. But God is a state of mind; one without needs: without fear, hunger, or pain. Needs are what make humanity imperfect and it is their body that creates them. Their path should be to separate themselves from their connection to this world, which is their body. Their path should be to make themselves pure."

He reclined back into his chair and waved his hand across his desk. "Have you paid no attention to what we are doing, to what we are building? Humanity is already immortal and when they find the rest of God, they will have no needs because then this world will only give and not take. 'God shall wipe away all tears from their eyes; and there shall be no more death, neither sorrow, nor crying neither shall there be any more pain: for the former things are passed away.'"9

I shook my head. "This world's only worth is as a mirror for humanity to self reflect and see their flaws; So that with willpower, they can recreate themselves into something closer to perfection. But you instead, want them to twist this mirror and build themselves a never-ending path of consumption and appetite. You would have them build their own chains and become slaves to this world. Humanity has the power of being so much more. What if they felt no hunger or thirst because they willed their bodies not to? "'Whosoever drinketh of the water that I shall give him shall never thirst; but the water that I will give him will become in him a well of water springing up to eternal life.'"10

I could see the aggravation in his face. "Slaves?! When they will have the power to destroy and build this world to how they see fit?

When they will manipulate it into their own translation of perfection? You call that slavery?

"If they are imperfect, what they will create can not be perfect. Whatever humanity makes is a reflection of themselves. They will only build a monument to their fears and needs. 'This people have sinned a great sin, and have made them gods of gold.'"11

I could see now that this was playing out exactly how I did not want it to. "God is not control. God is freedom. A glimpse of God would destroy your world, your Garden of Eden, and that is why it won't work."

The Levite simply shook his head and smiled. "I was hoping it wouldn't come to this, but you have become too dangerous." He pushed the button on the intercom on his desk. "Mr. Page please send the guards I had you bring up."

You could hear a moment of silence, then Mr. Page's response, "Yes Sir."

The Levite turned back to me. "Levites normally don't make contact with humans. We always influence them indirectly through speech and Michael. The use of guards is highly irregular." His tone was nonchalant.

"What about Miss. Debora, Mr. Dulant, and Mr. Page?"

He gave me an odd look and smiled. "It is as if you have no fear at all. Maybe you don't or maybe you're really good at masking it.

Debora, Dulant, and Page in a sense, were separated from humanity a long time ago. We chose them as mediators between the people and us. In turn, we granted them eternal being by simply continuing to clone them as they had been since our conception and allowed them to retain their memories of their past lives."

There was a knock on the Levite's door. "Come in Page." The Levite stood.

Mr. Page came in. His face distorted by confusion and sadness; he was accompanied by the guards. The Levite then began to walk out of the room and down the hall. We all followed. I did with a guard at each arm.

We boarded the same vehicle we had used to visit Michael.

When we entered I found that there was a modification made to one of the pipes that vented the viruses into the atmosphere. It had been redirected to the room in which I was explained Michael's true purpose. I was put in the room by the guards, after which, they promptly left.

The Levite walked up to the intercom that was on the door, this was also a new addition. "You made me work pretty hard these past couple of weeks. Since I am your only blind spot, this job fell completely on me. But in a matter of..." He looked down at his watch, "one hour and twenty seven minutes your new room will fill up with a virus I made for you. After this is done I will study you and see where I went wrong. I will then remake you and solve the problem." His words were blunt and sterile. "You will still be the one to lead the Elect to our true God. You are the last version of us necessary to complete this task."

I sat down and waited. After some time, I could feel the air coming in through the vents blow harder. I walked up to the door that had been reinforced and grabbed the handle.

The Levite watched, at first perplexed, but then began to laugh.

I continued pulling. I could feel the muscles in my arms and legs begin to tear. Disks in my spine began to compress then fracture. Still, I continued. The joints in my arms began to dislocate and my skin started to tear like a sheet of paper. The Levite stopped laughing and instead widened his eyes in disbelief as the door began creaking.

The door flew off. The door and I both fell back to the other side of the room. I pushed myself back and sat up against the wall.

The Levite's countenance had become serious. He walked towards my room. Mr. Page, who had tears rolling down his cheeks since we arrived at Michael, grasped the Levite's shoulder and called him by name.

"Jacob."

The Levite brushed off Mr. Page's hand without looking back and came in the room. He walked up and sat down in front of me. We both stared at each other for a moment. I was breathing heavily; my body was destroyed.

"When you had told me of the idea of separating mind from body through willpower you had already done it."

"Yes, I had to when I found myself. After my experience with death had separated me from the Elect I had to then separate myself from my body in order to find my mind. I can still feel everything, but since then I have been able to control it. I didn't tell you because after you gave me time to recuperate before we talked, I thought of the possibility of this outcome.

The Levite continued to stare, but his eyes began to dim. "You know this won't change anything. The thought of progress, of perfection, is embedded too deep in humanity. All you have succeeded in doing is set them back a few thousand years.

His voice was becoming weaker. "Don't you understand? If you were to annihilate everyone on earth except a pair, humanity would inescapably arrive at this exact same point. You, your god, could wipe them out again and again and it wouldn't make a difference." The Levite paused to muster what little strength he had for his next sentence. "As long as humanity exists my vision of heaven is inevitable, it is eternal."

I watched him. "I'm not trying to change this world. I'm trying to change their minds." After I finished speaking the Levite slumped over and died.

I sat there breathing hard. I had lost a lot of blood and the virus was slowly consuming me. With all my strength, I outstretched my arm to the Levite and touched his hand.

The Levite immediately gasped for air and in a look of bewilderment, he scuffled back using his feet and hands without taking his sight off of me.

I could no longer hold up my arm. "Humanity is defined by their psychology not their materialization on this earth... What if instead of controlling this world like gods, they were to think like God?" I let go and died.

Chapter 13

"What did you get for answer 56 on the test? I looked over at Edmund who was holding his paper to his face as we walked down the hall. This was the last class we had together for the day.

"Uhh," he scanned down the sheet. "56? Here we are, phosphorus."

"Phosphorus? Ha ha." I couldn't help but laugh.

"What's wrong with phosphorus for the answer?" He was beginning to look agitated.

"Nothing." I was still smiling. "As long as it's white." My smile grew bigger and I watched his face for the expression I had seen so many times before.

"Ahh! White phosphorus. I kept going back to that problem. I knew there was something wrong." He looked at it now, probably hoping he could turn back time.

"Alright, I'll see you later." We split in opposite directions to our next class. I looked back; he was still staring at that test.

"You know they're going to tell us our jobs tomorrow." He spoke, but didn't look up from his paper.

"I know."

"White phosphorus." He shook his head.

"Look it's tomorrow, we have had tests in every class today and have them in every class that's left. Don't worry about one question on one test." This didn't seem to help much. "Ok, I'm taking off, I don't want to be late.

"Alright." He began walking again.

I walked into my class and sat down. Miss. Ivanhiemer was placing the test on each desk. I sat down and waited for the rest of the students to come in. I looked around to see who was missing and saw Jacob sitting there, staring out of the window.

It always bothered me that I never saw him study. The only time I would see him open a book was when he first got it. He would only flip through it. Even Miss. Ivanhiemer only asked him a couple questions in the beginning of the class and after our first test, she never called on him again.

I always wondered if he was the reincarnation of either Mr. Dulant or Mr. Page. One thing is sure, Jacob is a prodigy like they are. Even though he's in a building full of the best minds, New Jerusalem has to offer, he instantly distinguished himself from among us. I've heard stories from other students in the beginning, in which Jacob answered highly complex problems instantly when called upon. After being told to show his work, it showed he had come up with formulas that made the ones being taught by the teacher obsolete.

"And start." Miss. Ivanhiemer's voice broke my train of thought. I took one last look at Jacob and saw him still staring out the window as if he hadn't heard a thing. Miss. Ivanhiemer, who would have scolded anyone else for not taking the test seriously, went to her desk and sat down as equally ignorant of Jacob's presence as he was of hers.

I took a deep breath to clear my mind and began.

After I finished I looked over all the answers and felt confident I had done well. Miss. Ivanhiemer walked around and collected the tests. I was about to leave when she tapped on her desk to get our attention.

"Tomorrow your jobs will be given to you in this class, be sure to be here on time... on time." (She always repeats what she wants to emphasize instead of doing it with her tone).

I went out and met Edmund near his classroom door. He was looking at another test he had received back with a fresh expression of confusion and frustration.

"Hey, Edmund. Guess what class I'm getting my job in."

"Ummm, Miss. Ivanhiemer's. It's obvious since you just came out of there before asking me." His eyes were still scanning his test.

"Yeah..." I stared at him. "Do you know what this means?" I pushed aside his test.

"No." He walked away a short distance and began looking over his papers again.

"I finally get to see who Jacob is."

"So?" He rolled up his test and put it in his back pocket.

"So!? Wouldn't it bother you if someone else always did much better than you without even trying."

Edmund shook his head. "I could say that about you, and yes it bothers me but I don't obsess about it."

"I'm not obsessing. Look there's a big difference from Jacob and me. I try. You and I have studied together before in the study hall; you've seen me."

I looked over and Edmund had his test out again. He shrugged, "Maybe he's a Levite."

"What? A Levite... it has been close to a thousand years."

"Alright, I'm going to my next class." Edmund stored his test once again and walked off.

I stood there. "A new Levite in my life time." It was a crazy idea but I still had a couple classes to attend to today before I could find out tomorrow.

Chapter 14

I went into Miss. Ivanhiemer's class first thing the next morning. It felt odd since it had been one of the last classes I attended in my daily schedule for years.

I entered and sat down. Miss. Ivanhiemer had a large pile of packets on her desk and was waiting attentively for everyone to take their place. After a moment she began passing them out. She began handing them at the corner of the room closest to me. I watched as each student that received his immediately began flipping through it.

Once she dropped the packet on my desk, I couldn't help feel how simple and ordinary it looked. My entire life was in this packet, both future and past, and it was summed up by a stack of paper with "Helio" in large font on its' cover.

I was about to open it when I remembered, Jacob. I looked over and saw that Miss. Ivanhiemer had skipped him and for the first time, I saw a look of confusion on his face. I looked over at the doorway and saw our building's director. He stood there for a moment and then gestured Jacob to follow him. Jacob stood up and left with him.

The whole room had gone silent by now. The flipping of pages and comparisons among students had ceased. We sat there and stared at the empty doorway. Miss. Ivanhiemer simply continued passing out packets, after she finished, she walked to the front of the class.

"Now that your jobs have been given to you, you will have the rest of the day to go over your past notes. Remember, your jobs have been chosen for you by the Levite in correspondence to your current gifts and potential. He demands much from us, but never more than what we can do. Hard work and learning from your past mistakes will help you reach your quotas. A few of you might even surpass them. We have much to learn from this world and much to do... much to do." Miss. Ivanhiemer paused, though I understood this would be the last time any of us would see her, she never showed much emotion. "You are dismissed."

I walked out with my packet. I didn't get a chance to even open it. I decided I would look over it with Edmund, who was probably currently stressing over the position he had been given and the prospect of reaching his life's quota.

I walked past a cluttered hall of students looking over their packets. Hall after hall was filled with the chattering and comparison of numbers and past lives. I walked out of the building to a patch of trees I sometimes studied under and found Edmund sitting on a bench; an expression of worry already on his face.

I walked up and sat down on the grass where I would study. "Hey."

"Hey."

"What did you get?" He was still looking over his packet.

"853 points and the job of molecular engineer."

"853 points out of 900 total. That's very impressive you're sure to get a managerial position."

I seemed more exited for the news than Edmund who's' countenance hadn't changed as he gave me the news.

"I probably will get a managerial position." Edmund let out a deep sigh. "But that would mean that not only will my life be judged by how close I get to my quota, but I will also be judged on how close my subordinates get to theirs."

"Your looking at this wrong," I smiled, but not because of what he said, simply because he was exactly as I had pictured him before I saw him. "The Levite has obviously put a great deal of confidence in you by giving you such a high number and by it, so many people under your direction. Do you think the Levite would be wrong?

"No." This seemed to uplift his spirits a bit. "I guess you're right." He put away his packet; he had been staring at the last page while I tried to cheer him up. "So, what did you get?"

"Oh, I haven't looked through my packet yet, I wanted to tell you something first."

"What?"

"Just hear me for a second. Do you remember Jacob?"

"Yeah."

"He didn't even get a packet." Edmund squinted at what I said. "Instead the director of our entire building showed up to escort him somewhere else."

"The director showed up personally? Where do you think he took him?"

He was obviously as surprised as I was. "I don't know, but it made me think... do you think he might really be a Levite?"

Edmund's eyes showed a deal of surprise with my suggestion, which made me think that he was only joking when he had suggested the idea himself.

"I don't know. A new one only comes around, what? Every thousand years now?"

"Yeah, I think so." We both sat silent for a moment. "Well, if he is, our current Levite will introduce him to us in the upcoming weeks. I guess we'll have to wait to know."

I looked down at my packet, that was next to one of the tree trunks. "Helio." I picked it up.

This got the attention of Edmund, who was still contemplating on either his newfound responsibility or the idea of living in a time where a new Levite would be introduced. "What did you get?"

The first page showed my number. I was shocked, "900."

"Nine... let me see that." Edmund took the packet and instantly looked crushed. "How could you have gotten 900? I've been listening to the other students on the way over here and my number has been the closest so far; it's not really close.

I took back my packet and flipped to the next page.

Edmund put his hand over his eyes, almost cringing as he spoke, "What job did you get?"

It was obviously the page where my job should be described because it had a list of my past work but what it said didn't make any sense.

I stared at it, "It says, Heaven."

Chapter 15

Edmund and I discussed what a job description of "Heaven" could possibly mean; again, we came to the same conclusion that only waiting would give me the answer.

It was understood that our jobs would be given to us today and that then tomorrow we would be separated into groups and sent off to new facilities where we would spend another portion of our lives being educated on our job's new, more specific, subjects. Those with the highest numbers would be separated from their groups and groomed for managerial positions.

It is our natural birth with its inherited strengths and weaknesses that determines what facility we begin in as children and what future job we receive. Those that are born with a high intelligence are placed in an advanced facility. Those that are not are placed, likewise, in a corresponding building.

The jobs that are given to us are influenced to an extent by our mental and physical inheritance but are determined by our abilities and characteristics that are fleshed out by our tests and classes.

Our numbers decide what job position we hold. Higher numbers outrank those with lower ones. Who we work with is predetermined so that a person of lower capability outranking others does not come up as an issue. Only those in managerial positions have a significant difference in mental or physical abilities compared to those they work with.

Our work in our past lives determines our number. The Levite, Our Sheppard, is the one who judges our mental and physical capacity a few years after our birth and then assigns us our classes, jobs, and our quota. How close we get to the assigned quota during the correlated lifetime is what determines our number during that life and the next.

Throughout our lives we don't know what our quota is. Our Shepherd is ahead of us in the path to God by thousands of years. So the portion of knowledge he has set for each individual to find is a part of the path the Levite has already been on. The Levite's job isn't to tell us the knowledge that makes up the path to God, but to guide us through it by giving us our jobs. This way, we walk the path ourselves.

Our quotas can't be told to us because the quota can be a new way of thinking, a new knowledge, an amount of work hours, or the discovery of a new technology. If we were told our quotas, it would defeat the purpose of having us walk the path ourselves.

The purpose of our numbers is that they represent our sincerity to the cause of building a heaven on earth. Regardless of the fact that in some cases simply telling someone their quota involves revealing something that would take hard work to find, in itself. Someone knowing what is expected from them and then achieving it, is much different than some one who achieves these almost impossible goals by their own will. It shows they do it not because they are told to, but because they see themselves capable of more. It is this mentality as a whole that guides us to God and heaven. Those with a higher number represent those who are closer to both, despite of their job and inherited limits. This is why they are given a managerial position and the burden to direct the rest since they are the closest.

Edmund's job, packet, and future made sense; mine did not. Humanity, obviously hasn't reached its goals. We don't know everything. In the end, the best Edmund and I could come up with was that it could be some form of rapture. Humanity hasn't reached God but maybe the Levite did... maybe I had done enough.

The next day students were taken from our dormitory to their new lives. In the end, only I was left. I sat on my bed not knowing what to expect.

I looked around. We only entered the dormitory when it was time to sleep. I had never seen it so empty; it had never looked so big. I watched the room's entrance from a distance. I had thought of sitting closer, but each student had his own space. Even though no one would be back, it seemed wrong for me to be in anyone else's space other than my own.

After some time, the door moved and in stepped a man with completely white hair. At first I didn't know what to think. His eyes seemed to be completely closed; an observation that startled me since he then instantly turned his face in my direction.

"You must be Helio."

"Yes Sir."

"Please follow me. I'll be taking you to your next job."

I stood up and took one last look at the gray and white room before exiting. I followed him out to the rail system where a group of people was waiting for us in one of the vehicles. I had never seen any of them before, but they all seemed to be my age. They looked as clueless as I was.

My guide walked in the vehicle. I went in as well and sat in an available seat. I looked around and found everyone staring in my direction. After a moment, probably because I was looking at them with the same expression that they were at me, they realized I didn't know anything they didn't and quickly lost interest.

Across from me sat a slender girl with pale hair that almost looked white. She had large blue eyes that drew my attention when I looked at her face. I leaned over, "Did anyone else come out of that building other than me?"

She had been looking out at the trees when I asked her. She slowly turned her head from the panorama, which I could now clearly see she had been enjoying. I felt guilty for disturbing her. I was going to apologize but was drawn once again to her eyes. She noticed I had begun to form a sentence and waited, which created an awkward pause.

"I'm sorry, I didn't realize you were concentrating." I could feel my face turn red.

She smiled, I wasn't sure if it was as an acceptance to my apology or because of the color of my face. "Its alright. I'm Rota."

I had been completely rude. I hadn't introduced myself, yet I still asked something of her. "Oh. I'm Helio."

"Nice to meet you." she smiled once again. I felt utterly embarrassed. "Well, let me see. It went him then her then her then him." After a moment she muttered to herself and continued pointing at the different passengers in the order they had boarded until her finger landed on me. "No, she was from a different building." Her finger landed once again on the person chronologically before me.

I couldn't help but stare; her wide eyes closed half way every time she spoke. I found myself concentrated on this mannerism rather than the response to my question.

We stopped and our guide moved to the front of the vehicle. He stood in front of an enormous transparent dome. It looked to be made of glass or crystal, but neither material seemed capable of bending light so drastically.

We all stood in awe.

Our guide stretched out his hand in the direction of the enormous dome in a theatrical motion, "Heaven." He gave a crooked smile as a response to our stupefied looks, and then began the vehicle again.

When the vehicle had stopped we were only able to see the peak of the dome, the horizon had obscured its' base; as we continued to approach it, an idea of the size of this structure began to sink into my mind. We were traveling at a high speed, yet the distance between us didn't seem to change.

"It's fifteen hundred miles wide by fifteen hundred miles long by fifteen hundred miles high, at its' pinnacle. The dome is a field we still don't yet understand but it is necessary to control the climate within." Our guide informed us as he faced this colossal structure. "We'll be there in a few hours."

I kept staring at the dome. It still didn't seem that we had gained any ground. And who was this man? He had said, "A field we don't yet understand," only the Levite knew things which humanity did not. Had this man had direct contact with the Levite himself?

"Excuse me Sir. I don't mean to be rude or forward, but may I ask you your name?" I had to know if my suspicions were correct.

He didn't say anything at first and only gave me a crooked smile. "You figured it out, didn't you? I was planning of making a game of it, a game which would have had a more interesting ending if another other than you had finished it." He took a bow, "Dulant, at your service."

There was a collective gasp in the vehicle. Mr. Dulant was one of the three clones, one of the three founders and most overwhelming of all he was one of the only three direct contacts to the Levite. All three: Mr. Page, Mrs. Debora, and Mr. Dulant represented the peak of human capability. Some say that they were engineered by the Levite after his appearance, and that they were made to such a mental point so that they could understand and carry out the Levite's orders. Given that they are partly credited with founding our society, I have always believed that this was just a rumor to explain their extraordinary skills and the gap between them and us.

Something was clear now. Whatever this "Heaven" is, it has been dictated by the Levite, and Mr. Dulant, who represents the Levite, has been sent by him to gather us and bring us to this structure.

Mr. Dulant took a seat in the front and only watched the dome slowly grow in size, seemingly a little disappointed.

I looked at them both with a wonder of a child who had seen the tales of his childhood come to life. I had pictured them in my mind when we were told of them but now that I saw them in person, they seemed more unreal than any fantasy my mind could have conjured.

Chapter 16

After some time we could see the base of the dome, which was a square. It had three gates that faced us, they were bright white and had a sort of large scanner over each door. The walls from which the field projected off the tops of, had a foundation made of different materials each one of a different color.

Mr. Dulant stood up and began explaining the base, much the same as when we first had seen the top of the dome. "There are twelve gates in total around Heaven, each one is made of a solid pearl. Above each gate there are scanners, appendages of Michael, that make sure only those who have been chosen are able to enter. The dome uses the sun's radiation to keep a constant temperature inside. It can do this during the night as well, because of its height. The Levite filled in the holes necessary to create this heaven, but it was mostly made from the gathered knowledge from across the world.

Since we had seen the base, though our speed hadn't changed, the distance between the dome and us was being closed quickly. I could now see that each material that made up the foundation had an inscription on it. I took a better look at the scanners above the gates, and could see inscriptions on them as well. They gave me a new sense of interest, appendages of Michael? Michael was described as omnipresent, and seeing pieces of it was confusing. The vehicle stopped.

"Here we are," said Mr. Dulant as he exited the vehicle. He walked forward and looked up at the gates, we were all instinctively doing the same. Pointing our chins to the sky, we strained to see the tops in which the scanners were perched.

With his hands in his pocket Mr. Dulant took a few steps back and began walking to the vehicle again, "Alright, this is where we part."

"But you haven't told us what we are supposed to do, what is our job?" A boy with curly hair had asked what we were all thinking.

Mr. Dulant kept walking and after he had entered the vehicle he turned around near its doorway to face us. "You can do whatever you want to do. In fact, that's your job. You don't even have to enter heaven if you don't want to."

The vehicle began to speed away from us. We could see Mr. Dulant take a seat at the end of the vehicle that faced us. I could no longer see the expression on his face but I could almost feel his smirk, after a moment, only the vehicle was distinguishable.

We all turned back to the gates. After looking around I began walking towards the middle one. Everyone had simultaneously done the same. As we got closer the gate began to open.

There was a gust of wind that escaped from the inside; the atmosphere within was different. We climbed twelve steps that were made up of twelve different precious stones to the entrance. Inside we found that there was an entire city; an entire city made of gold. The setting sun reflected off the mirror finish of the buildings blinding us as we entered.

Inside the clarity and warmth of the atmosphere made it seem as if it was the middle of the day. The radiation the dome was capturing was creating the changes in the light and climate.

I looked around, God, Truth, had created this, and the pursuit to find him had made this place possible.

The first thing we all did was split apart and investigated whatever had managed to catch our eye.

I began walking towards a rail vehicle that looked similar to the one we had arrived in, except it was solid gold.

It wasn't so much that this rail vehicle had piqued my interest but rather the possibility of specific locations being denoted in its list of destinations.

My suspicions were confirmed as I flipped through the different options on its screen. Among them were places with descriptions of different climates, sea level, and several dispensaries. Eventually, I came across a large map with a scale depiction that showed these points of interest along with nine other gates that opened to the outside world. Most interesting of all, there was a large place in the center marked as, "Tower." I had made up my mind. This would be the first place I would investigate in this "Heaven."

I began placing in my destination when I noticed Rota. She was strolling between buildings as if she were walking through a forest. She didn't pause, but glanced inside each window that she happened to pass.

I looked over at the screen and then back to Rota; who was now being obscured by a building. I waited a moment until she appeared again.

"Rota." She looked over without changing her pace.

"Yes?"

"Have you seen anything interesting?"

"Yes." She stopped and looked similar to when I had asked her a question before, "No flowers, no grass, no trees." During her answer her half open eyes wandered. "What are you doing?"

"I'm going to look at a tower at the center of this place." The word Heaven didn't come naturally to my lips as I spoke.

"What's so special about this tower?" Rota began walking again in the same pace as before, only this time she began looking at the rail vehicle.

"I don't know?" It was a good question. "It seemed as good a place as any to start looking... What was in those buildings?"

She closed her eyes and continued walking alongside the rail vehicle using only the feeling of her fingertips being run across its surface as her guide. "A couch, a table, chairs... things waiting for more people."

I smiled. I had never met someone like her. She had a peculiar presence that commanded my entire attention. "Do you want to join me?"

Why was I so nervous?

She opened her eyes and looked up at me, "To see the Tower?"

Her blue eyes were so large, "Yes."

She got on the vehicle and stood next to me as she pointed out to the distance. "To see, that tower?"

There was a peak out in the distance that seemed to hold up the dome that enclosed this place. By the look of it, it could not be anything else rather than the tower shown in the vehicles map. The thought that something roughly seven hundred and fifty miles away could be seen with the naked eye above the horizon, never crossed my mind.

I looked over at her and smiled, "Thank you, for joining me. But, what about a closer look?"

She chuckled and sat down, "I'm sorry. Yes I would love to."

There was a pause in which my eyes were drawn to hers. After a moment, I noticed and looked away to finish inputting our destination into the vehicles computer.

I sat opposite to her, similar to when we were first heading to this place, after the standard period of wait the vehicle began its course.

Rota looked at the scenery but she didn't seem as engrossed with the panorama as before. Gold building after gold building passed by in a blur. Rota looked over at me, "What did they teach you in your building?"

"Just general subjects like math, physics, chemistry and biology." A particularly wide gold wall reflected the back of Rota and the vehicle for a flash as we sped along. "What did they teach you?"

"The same subjects. The only thing I can see that is still natural is the sky, but I don't know anything about it."

Everything here is man made. Our ride reinforced this observation, though for some reason, the barrier that distorted its outer edges left the sky above us unchanged. Because of the stars and planets that were visible above us, I could tell that the sun had set completely outside of the dome, even though everything around us was as clear as day.

Rota seemed disillusioned by this absence. It seemed she was hoping to find some sort of plants or wild life closer to the center of Heaven, but there weren't any.

"They didn't teach me about the sky either." There was an air of melancholy about her as she looked up at it. I thought for a moment, "That group of stars sort of looks like a bird facing the moon."

Rota looked over at me with her eyes half closed, barely showing her pupils, and scrunched her eyebrows.

I started feeling my face turn red as I progressively became more nervous. However there was nothing I could do, I had already committed. "Uh, see it looks like he pecked it into a crescent since he couldn't reach the rest." I began to rub the back of my head and could barely look her in the face from the corner of my eyes.

She looked up again taking with her a gaze a tremendous weight off of me and looked back at the sky. "Oh, yeah I see it. It does look like that." She sat back down.

We both sat for a while without saying anything. My impromptu observation seemed to have the effect I hoped for, but I still felt embarrassed. After sometime, I looked up and found Rota looking at me.

"Thank you Helio."

My eyes widened a bit and I looked away.
"Your welcome."

Chapter 17

After a while we arrived at the tower. We looked around to see if anyone else had the same idea as us but found no one.

I looked over at Rota. She was looking at the entrance. It was a large red door with a four by three grid of precious stones imbedded in it. They were the same twelve stones that made up the foundation of Heaven. "Did you want to go in or wait for the rest to show up?"

I hadn't finished my sentence before Rota began to open the door. Inside were thousands of monitors similar to the ones I had used in my classes and to those that controlled the rail vehicles we used. Against the walls there were two stairways opposite of each other. Because of the cylindrical shape of the tower the two stairways looked like a double helix of a DNA strand.

I walked up to one of the monitors that turned on before I touched it. The screen read Helio. The font and an unassuming simplicity reminded me of my packet. I browsed over the different categories that came up. There were thousands upon thousands of options, all were different fields of study. There was biology, chemistry and so many others that I contented myself with quickly scrolling through the large list in order to get an impression of its length rather than reading each specific subject.

There were several choices though each ones label seemed very broad. I chose mathematics since I believed myself particularly well versed on the subject and felt I had a better chance of comprehending whatever this place happened to show me. Mathematics led me to other choices: subtraction, addition, multiplication, and division. Simple subjects, the highest of which I was well beyond in understanding.

I back tracked to the original menu and began browsing in alphabetical order. This time, taking my time to look at each specific subject. I stopped at astronomy and looked over at Rota. There was a glare in her eyes that reflected her screen. On her monitor there was a constant stream of different images running at an almost unrecognizable speed. Her finger was millimeters away from the screen as she stared at it with her eyes wide open.

I walked over to her, followed by the turning on and off of monitors as I came close to one and then passed it. Before reaching Rota, I opened my palm close to the surface of the next screen to turn it off.

"How did you get it to do that?"

"I just chose one of the subjects."

I looked at the flashing screen; the monitor's interface apparently is customized for each of us. "What did you choose?"

"Music. I can hear it in my head." She then tapped her screen with a speed that seemed more of a muscle reflex than a conscious action. The volley stopped at a page that read Johann Sebastian Bach Suite for Solo Cello No. 1 in G Major. Instinctively, I began reading the information presented on the screen when Rota, after a few more taps, vanished it. I looked up at her. She smiled, shook her head, and pointed to her ear, in a few seconds the room was filled with the sound of an instrument I had never heard before. I looked around at the high ceilings trying to locate its source, but the entire place seemed to reverberate with the tone. I looked at the yellowish gold walls; the black monitors, the red door and then back to Rota.

She was still smiling. My eyes were drawn to hers once again. As we stood there in the presence of this music, for the first time since we had arrived, since I could remember, the word beautiful hung at the edge of my lips. It was as if she had shared a feeling, a moment with me, rather than information.

The music came to an apex then slowly dissipated as it ended. We were still looking at each other, after a moment we both looked back to the screen. I exhaled. It seemed I had been unconsciously holding my breath the entire time.

I tried to make my deep breaths afterwards as inconspicuous as I could. I looked over at Rota,

I wanted to say something, anything, even though I didn't know what.

I turned to her struggling to find the words, "Rota I ... "

The door to the tower opened. The rest of our group had apparently found their way here, probably after noticing the tower in the skyline.

"Wow, what are all these monitors?"

"Look it says your name on the screen."

"Didn't we already study these?"

"Which ones are you looking at?"

After a moment Rota looked back at me. "Did you want to tell me something?"

My eyes were still on the others. "Uh, yeah, I just wanted to tell you that I was going to look at what the other levels have."

"OK, I'm still not done looking through these files."

She turned back to her screen and I waved to her as I began walking to one of the stairways.

The second floor looked exactly the same as the first. It seemed to have the same amount of monitors. I couldn't tell for sure since they were easily several thousands of them.

I searched the room but still found nothing different except the exclusion of the front door from the first floor. I decided that the difference had to be in the monitors themselves.

I walked up to one as before, and in the same way the monitor turned on before I reached it. "Helio."

I scanned the options and found Mathematics. This time the math lessons started where the monitor on the first floor left off. These new categories were still familiar to me, but they gave me an idea that seemed to be the obvious answer to what I would find in the continuing levels of the tower. I scaled up to the next level and went through the same protocol as before. I found that once again this level contained the mathematical progression of the anterior. I still knew these teachings.

I climbed higher; skipping levels and found completely new branches of mathematics I hadn't heard of before.

I could continue learning for the rest of my life on the subject of math alone, reflecting on the extraordinary height of the tower.

On the same level, I chose astronomy and saw that it mentioned other subjects as prerequisites, which were: the last branches of astronomy taught in the lower levels and previous math and physics classes. I decided to choose it regardless of my shortcomings.

As I looked through the lessons, I felt more and more lost. It made references to what I assumed were celestial bodies due to their context. And with these came a list of names of physic laws and mathematical theories that seemed to prove other vague concepts I couldn't make out.

I faced my palm toward the monitor once again and sat down. This tower seems to have all of the knowledge humanity has been able to gather. Each level of the tower is built on top of other broader ones, like the teachings each level has inside.

Each lower level contains lessons necessary to proceed to the ones above. Mankind's accession through knowledge. "What an odd place."

I decided to go back to the first level with a subject in mind. As I descended, I walked by some of the others that were on their way to find out what I had. When I got to the bottom I saw Rota in the same place. I turned on my monitor and began my first lesson.

Chapter 18

Our excitement of our first day resulted in us forgetting to introduce ourselves. We had even forgotten to find a dispensary for our food. After a brief introduction of ourselves to the group we all walked about and found a place for food. We were all accustomed to the interaction with the dispensary.

Something in our bodies would communicate with the machine and in turn it would give us a certain amount of pills that contained the refined substances we needed at the moment for nourishment. However there was an extensive list of things none of us had heard of that were available as well. In it were some recognizable things, such as clothing and shoes; but most of them were unrecognizable. As we all searched through the list, to everyone's surprise, a girl in our group let out a loud scream followed by, "Bicycle."

She began pressing the word on the screen repeatedly but nothing happened. I assumed this word: "Bicycle" was something she had read about in the tower. Whatever it was, the lack of reaction by the dispensary put her in a sad mood for the rest of the day.

We all decided to sleep close to the tower since we all planned on continuing some lesson or other the next day. I asked Rota to join me on the roof of one of the buildings. Once on top, we sat down.

"I wanted to show you something," I pointed towards the sky. "You see those bright stars that seem to form a ladle?"

"Where?"

"Right there." I pointed at the sky. She got closer to me to get a better look at where I was pointing. My heart began racing.

"Oh yeah, I see it.

"That's called The Big Dipper, it's part of a larger constellation called the Ursa Major.

"Ursa Major?"

"Yeah, but the interesting part I found is that if you take those two stars that are at the end of the ladle, opposite to the handle, you can connect the two with a line that will show you where a star called Polaris is."

"Is there something special about Polaris?"

"Yes, thousands of years ago it was also known as the North Star since ancient navigators used it as the general direction of true north."

"Can that still be done?"

"No, since the earths axis has a slight wobble, true north no longer points toward it. Our North Star is that one, Vega, its part of a constellation called Lyra.

We had slowly gone to our elbows and then laid down as we looked up and I was describing what I had learned.

As I pointed at the sky and spoke I could feel Rota looking over at me. After some time I looked over at her; we stared at each other and she smiled.

"How do you think these constellations got their name, Helio?"

"Well, these stars have always been there. Over time, the natural thing for humans to do has always been to name and categorize things so that they can try and understand them. It makes sense that people would use things they are familiar with here on earth to describe what they see in the sky. Like a bear for Ursa Major and a lyre for Lyra." Rota smiled and looked back up to the sky.

"What should we name our hungry bird?"

Hungry bird? I looked back at her. Then to the poorly depicted bird drawn out by a few stars I had pointed out previously. I had crammed my mind with so many facts I had forgotten about it. "I don't know... I think you should name it."

Rota stared at it for a while, "I don't know how the moon would taste but it is much larger than him."

Her description made me smile. "It's a him?"

Her face was still serious with concentration. "I don't know why but it looks like a him... how about Gourmand?"

"I think it's perfect."

We lied there and spoke of the night sky until it turned day. Though in Heaven, it never turned dark enough so that it could be called night; regardless of how the sky looked above it.

The next day we all went to the dispensary once again; and again the same girl gave the same piercing yell as before. Only this time we all silently joined in her astonishment. What I presume was the Bicycle she attempted to acquire yesterday was lying against the dispensary.

She quickly ran to it and propped it up. What she would do next with it was a complete mystery to us all. She then sat on it and after slightly rotating the wheels by manipulating the pedals with her feet she promptly fell over. We all watched in awe. She had conveyed the general function of the Bicycle even though it was poorly executed. She went through the whole motion of attempting, once again. The rest crowded the dispensary to scour through what now had become a wish list.

I stood there. There was nothing I wanted. Rota looked at the machine with some interest, but didn't walk over to it until after the others had finished placing their orders.

Fueled by what we had discovered in the tower, the dispensary and the description of the different locations in the rail vehicle's atlas, we all split up once again and began exploring "Heaven."

Rota and I explored for several days until we came to a building with a particularly large roof and decided to make it our home. The days afterwards were filled with the task of finding furniture. There were endless varieties of styles and types of furniture to choose from. We had all grown up with the same simplistic style of accommodations. So our choices were almost absurd. When we finished we looked at our eclectic collection of color, lines and style, and were happy.

I continued studying the sky fueled by Rota's smile and the time we spent together on the roof of our house. I would point out the location of a new constellation, star, planet, asteroid or comet, and she would scrunch up her eyes and stare in the direction I pointed. Afterwards, we would lay there for hours conversing on what other places of "Heaven" we would go to next or what subject had interested us in the tower which we wanted to continue learning. It didn't matter what we spoke of, what made me happy was that I was with her and she was with me.

From the first day we looked over the constellations Rota and I had poured our minds into one another. We knew everything there was to know about each other, except one thing that I could never get out of Rota. She would disappear randomly and reappear during the day. I would ask her about it, but she would only change the subject and smile.

This continued for a few years until one day, in almost an unbridled excitement, she woke me up and told me she was ready to show me what she had been up to. She pulled and tugged at my arms as I got ready. Rota was dressed as if she had just awoken even though she was clearly wide-awake. She ran out and I followed confused; we got on the rail vehicle and she covered the vehicle's screen while she inputted the coordinates and sat down in front of me.

"Did you go to your place that you're always disappearing to today?"

She only sat there, looked at me and smiled.

After some time I realized we were headed towards the tower. She clearly read this on my face and her smile grew larger.

Once we went in, Rota sat me down in my chair and walked behind me.

"Don't look over, not yet."

I could hear the sound of something being picked up and moved; the sound of her sitting and then adjusting herself in her seat.

There was a long pause. Meanwhile, my mind was running the sounds I had heard through my mind over and over again, trying to piece together a faint clue of what was going on.

Then I heard the sound of a Cello; it was Johann Sebastian Bach's Suite for Solo Cello No. 1. The same song Rota and I had heard together. I turned around a saw that Rota was the one playing the song. She sat in a chair barefoot and in her gown with her white skin in a light pink hue from her excitement.

I was mesmerized. Her eyes were looking down at the bow as she moved it back and forth. She looked up and I saw that her eyes were half open, the same as when she spoke. I stared into them and found myself lost in her tune as my body shivered. I watched the song coming through her, a vibration of her soul. It was as if she was uttering a word of God, and though I could not comprehend it, I could feel it inside of me. The feeling was not of this world. My vague sense of perfection had been made tangible, visible, whole, and though it confronted me my conventional senses could not describe it. Rota had not only found it within herself, but was sharing it with me.

I could see beads of sweat begin to form on her body. She looked at me once again and smiled as she played the last notes.

After she had finished, I didn't know what to say. What could anyone say? I had been raptured and then dropped. It wasn't the song alone. It was the time she had devoted, it was what that song had meant to us, but most of all she had showed me her heart; fragile, pure, vulnerable. It was the most beautiful thing I had ever seen, If I were given a lifetime in the tower, I would not find the words to respond with.

She walked over and hugged me. We held each other and time itself, seemed to stop.

Chapter 19

Years passed and we remained the same. We walked through Heaven when the sun was visible in the dome's opening and we would lie down on a roof and look at the stars when they appeared.

Rota learned different songs and played her Cello sporadically. It was something I always looked forward to where ever we were. I had nothing to give her as precious as her music was for me. However, I continued learning about the sky and as I progressed higher in the tower's levels, what I learned became more technical. I no longer learned of subjects categorized and explained by things as simple as ancient gods and earthly objects. Things became pure manifestations of control. Mathematical equations and physical laws governed the cosmos. The mastery of these allowed an individual to take the complexity of the heavens and restrain them in the meek boundaries of paper. The sky was no longer as magical and mysterious as when Rota and I had found Gourmand.

After time passed, it seemed to me that Rota was growing weaker. I would ask her about it, but she would change the subject. This continued for some time until her condition became undeniable.

We walked about the buildings after she had suggested a challenge as to which of us could find the ugliest piece of furniture in heaven.

We decided to make it a game of chance by taking turns being the first to look inside each new building we came across. Thanks to an exceptional piece I had found several buildings ago, I had given up my turns to Rota, confident that I had won.

I watched her as she walked up to a building and covered her eyes with her hands before she got too close and then opened them quickly to look inside. After a moment, she would scrunch her eyes and continue walking to the next. Afterwards, I would follow and look inside as well; my specimen was formidable indeed.

It was during this course that she began to stagger. She reached out to grasp the edge of a window but fell to her knees. When I saw this, I ran to help her but came to a pause as a horror enveloped me when I looked at her.

She had her hands cupped beneath her face catching droplets of blood. My heart began to palpitate; my mind was tearing itself with what to do as I watched this crimson pool grow in her porcelain hands.

Rota looked up at me. As she did, a droplet ran down her face and outlined her mouth. I looked into her eyes; my mind almost at a point of bewilderment. Her expression wasn't of fear, but what I read was pity.

"Rota please tell me what's going on. Please!" I could not control the sound of my voice and that last of my words came out in a sorrowful tone.

She began to stand up. I quickly grasped her hands to help her. We went inside and sat down. I insisted she lie down but she shook her head.

Rota looked more collected, but only sat there looking at her hands with her fingers interlaced. She gave a deep sigh. "I'm sorry I hadn't told you before, but I didn't want this to loom over everything we did."

"What is it?" I was doing what I could to keep myself from panicking.

She kept looking at her hands; the blood on them had become dark. I thought of when I helped her up and the idea of her blood darkening on my skin came to mind. I will not look. I couldn't look. I was at the edge of an abyss and I had to keep myself together.

She took a deep breath and looked at me. I was not seeing the reassurance I was hoping for. "Helio... I'm going to die. Soon."

"Why? No! This isn't true, this can't be true!" I began pacing the room. "There isn't supposed to be death in Heaven, isn't that what the Bible says?" I clenched my fists as hard as I could.

"There isn't death. I'll come back. I'll only be gone for a little while." I could hear her get up and walk towards me.

I kept looking down. I didn't want to look at her. I was about to break. The hold I had on my feelings were about to sever. I felt like I had to be strong for Rota. I wouldn't forgive myself if I couldn't do something for her because I couldn't control myself.

She placed her hand on my cheek and lifted my face to hers. "Please don't let this ruin the time we still have together. You still have another hundred years at least. I'll come back. I'll join you again and we will pick up where we left off."

She said it to console me, but it did nothing. Rota had something I had never seen in anyone else.

"I thought every disease had been cured," An anger rose in me as I spoke. Anger arose in me toward my teachers, society, and the Levite. They had lied to me. I opened my hands and looked at them. "Why would they say that? Why is this happening?"

Rota covered my hands with hers. "I was born with a genetic disease. A disease that affects parts of my Adam and Eve DNA. If they cured me, I wouldn't be me anymore. It would have affected my psychology, so they did nothing. I was told about it and raised with a few others in a similar situation. I hadn't met someone my age that was normal until Mr. Dulant segregated us; then I met everyone here, and I met you."

We looked at each other for moment. A gamut of feelings was tearing me up inside while I tried to look collected.

"Please Helio, don't let fear control our lives. I want to be with you and you wouldn't be you if you let this overshadow you."

"I think your asking more than I can bear. The most precious thing I have here is the time I spend with you. Now your telling me it's going to be cut short and there's nothing I can do but watch you die?"

I saw the expression that my words had caused and it cut me deeper than what fate had given her. Rota truly believed that death would only be a small lapse in time and I would never want her to feel what I was feeling at that moment.

"I think this is probably coming in to fast. Everything will be alright. I'll wait for you; we still have time." She studied my eyes. Maybe because she saw something within me I couldn't find myself, so that I could believe what I had told her, She smiled.

That night, we watched the stars together like we always did and I told her of what I had learned. Rota fell asleep with her head against my chest as we laid on the rooftop.

I waited and after a while I gently held her head and slipped away from her. I went inside and there, broke down; I couldn't hold it in anymore. Tears ran down my face uncontrollably. I felt powerless. Rota, my world, was falling apart in front of me and there was nothing I could do.

I fell on my knees and begged, "Please Levite, I know you can hear me, please save her. You can do anything you want; please do this. I know your understanding is beyond me but I don't ask this because I know better, it is because I have nothing else. I have nothing else and I have nothing to stop it. Please Levite, please!"

Days passed and my desperate crys went unanswered. Rota became thinner and weak. I watched her become a shadow of who she was. I still loved her with all my heart. Though her body degraded, mentally she acted as if nothing was happening. She still insisted on visiting different parts of Heaven. I had to help her walk since she could no longer do it under her own strength.

There came a day in which we couldn't go out anymore. Rota's symptoms were effecting her more and more often. It was this day that she asked me for her Cello. I hadn't heard her play in weeks; now it was a request that only made me fear for her health rather than bring me happiness.

She insisted and I gave it to her.

"I don't have much time Helio. I wrote us a song that I wanted to play for us. It was going to be a secret celebration of mine if I turned out to be ok, but now I want to play it while I still have the chance. It's a song you made possible Helio. I was able to make this song because of the feelings I have for you.

She sat up on the edge of the bed and held up the Cello. I was sitting next to her and nearly stood up to help her. I thought she was going to fall over with the weight of her instrument. I settled back down and she began.

Her rhythm was cheerful and quick, a perfect reflection of her personality. Rota continued this way for some time, changing the tempo but not the tone. Afterwards, she transitioned to a lower tone; the rhythm remained similar to the first. It was still upbeat, but not as much. She looked up at me as she played it. She did the same with this tone as she had done with the first and changed the beat. Rota continued this for a while and then began transitioning from one tone to another; each with its own rhythm. Her pace began to quicken and the transition between each tone became shorter and shorter.

She was sweating profusely but instead of slowing down, she took a deep breath, closed her eyes and sped up. The two tones together made a completely different song. When her performance peaked, it sounded as if two people were playing and intertwining two different songs at the same time.

I watched her and couldn't hold back my tears. Her song was breaking my soul, but I couldn't look away. There she sat; years of practice gave her a talent that her disease couldn't touch. She continued, making both ethereal bodies of sound dance together. And there I was, her giving me the greatest gift I have ever been given, and I powerless to help her, to do anything. I felt completely pathetic in her presence.

Rota finished and handed me her Cello. She sat panting for air and sweating. Then she did something that crushed what little perception of strength I had left of myself. She looked into my eyes and with a weakness I hadn't heard in her before she said, "Thank you Helio."

Rota had held me by the hand and showed me a beauty I would have never even recognized if she hadn't described it to me with her music; and she was thanking me?

We went to the roof that night as we always did. I tried to change Rota's mind so she would stay in bed. I wanted to have as much time as possible with her as I could. But she wanted to see the stars.

We lied there and watched the sky. Rota and I had always talked for hours before we slept and I couldn't think of anything to say. "She is slipping away," was the only thing I could think. I knew she was close to dying. I felt it as if it were a cancer that was eating me inside, leaving a husk.

Her voice brought me out of my thoughts. "Helio." She had her hand outstretched towards me. Immediately I held it. "Helio tell me a story about the stars, please like before. Lets pretend at least for a moment as if nothing was wrong and talk like we used to.

I took a deep breath and stared at the sky for a moment. "There once was a child who was shown Heaven here on earth." I squeezed her hand, holding the very thing I had seen. I made an effort to compose myself. "This boy spent the rest of his life searching the skies for an explanation of what he saw here on earth. You see, this boy was given a great gift and wished to repay the person who had given it to him." I could feel her grip becoming weaker. "He looked above him to try to find words that could possibly describe what he had felt so that he could make that person understand how precious she was to him; to let her understand how grateful he was." Her hand became limp in mine. "This boy never found what he looked for, where he looked. I'm sorry Rota I was never able to find the words."

I saw that she had stopped breathing. Her eyes were wide open and staring at the sky. I put her palm to my face and sobbed like a child.

Chapter 20

The next day I took her body on the rail vehicle. I had no more tears. A part of me was dead and I no longer felt anything. I came to the west gates. Their splendor, meticulous detail, and grandeur went unnoticed as I crossed them. I looked only at what I held.

When I crossed the gateway I felt the grass underneath my feet and the sun on my face. I found a space underneath the largest tree and with one of its dead branches I began digging. It took me hours. The ground was hard and my hands became bloody with my efforts, but my mind was disconnected to the pain. It had become dark when I placed her into the earth. I lay on the grass besides her staring at the night sky. I laid there all night and the next day I placed her Cello on her grave.

"I'm sorry Rota, I wish I could believe that you'll come back. But I'll never see you again on this earth. I could be made thousands of times because what I know can be taught. The God you had inside isn't a God that can be manipulated or controlled. No one can use your God to bring you back, our society can't teach what they don't know and haven't seen." I looked towards the Tower. "There's something I still have to do, but one day I'll join you again."

I crossed the gates again and got on the rail vehicle. I headed toward the tower with the intent of climbing it.

Once I got there, I avoided looking over to Rota's computer but caught a glimpse of it with the corner of my eye before I could control myself completely. I got to the stairs and began; I knew it would be a long task, a tower that could be seen from seven hundred and fifty miles away.

The work was monotonous. I looked down at my feet as each one ascended to take the next step. My mind was blank and I concentrated only on walking. Only the sound of my progress registered in my mind. I had become an automaton looking for something that would justify my existence.

Days went by and I continued. I passed identical room after identical room and only the motion of my feet reassured me that I was heading in the right direction.

My unrelenting rhythm paid off and I reached a door on the ceiling. I opened it and found gusting winds and the blinding sun on the other side. It took me a moment for my eyes to adjust and look around.

I found nothing.

There was only a complete view of "Heaven;" all its gilded glory, its borders, and the twelve gates. My fatigue, hunger, thirst, and disappointment came down on me all at once. The weight of it on my shoulders pushed me to the ground.

I didn't know what I was looking for, but it wasn't this.

Between my hands on the floor I saw a distorted reflection of myself on the gold floor. I stared into my warped image and watched it mouth the words I spoke. "This is what this place has to offer."

I stood up and walked to the edge of the tower, stepping one of my feet half way off the edge. I stared at the geometric shapes the clusters of buildings formed as I thought of how the others here in "Heaven" had set their lives. They created mental and physical competitions with what they learned and used time to separate the winners. They did this time and time again, building, climbing the Tower within themselves. It all seemed so pointless now.

I looked over to where I had buried Rota. The ground was distorted by "Heaven's" barrier and for the first time since her death, a feeling came over me. It was one of pure hatred and rage of what this place really was.

"Are you happy Levite?! Are you happy with your test? Did you get the data you hoped for?!" I was yelling as hard as I could. "Was this my job? To live in this petty place and watch the only thing that was pure die in front of me?!" It was the only time I had spoken to him since I pleaded for Rota's life.

"Let me die Levite! Erase me from this earth. You did nothing to save her at least this way I'll have a chance of seeing her again."

The tears in my eyes blurred my panorama as the thought of this improbable chance slowly turned my hate to sorrow.

"I could have been happy Rota. This place, would have been Heaven to me if you hadn't opened my eyes; if you hadn't shared with me your heart."

Bibliography

King James Bible, 1. Proverbs 2:2-5, 2. Mathew 7:7-8, 3. Luke 9:62, 4. Mathew 7:18, 5. Luke 12:2, 6. Proverbs 3:19, 7. Isaiah 9:2, 8. Leviticus 21:21, 9. Revelations 21:4, 10. John 4:14, 11. Exodus 32:31.

Acknowledgements

I would like to thank my friends Michael Callos, Jessica Callos, Jose Perez, Gina Perez, and Frank Dorritie.

I have found through my short time in this life that this world is full of mirrors. There are very few that reflect the truth. I am fortunate to have found friends, that with their honesty, have allowed me to see truths about myself, which have enabled me to improve who I am and my work. I sincerely thank you.

To Kassandra Limon, your natural talents and skills have outshined me at a young age. I hope you find a path worthy of your potential. Thank you for helping me when I most needed it.

Para mis padres, Antonio y Camerina Delgadillo. Gracias por siempre apoyarme en cualquier cosa que me he propuesto hacer. Siempre han sido mi base.

A special thanks to my high school English teacher Mr. Haley. Your interpretation of literature and passion for this art revealed a whole new world for me. I never found your depth of insight in any other teacher. I hope this book finds you one day and you will critique it; because I know you will see it for what it is.

Last, thank you Ashley Miller for the anxiety you gave me. This book was an attempt to erase it.